Saving Santa's Seals

To Felix,

Follow Your
Dreams!!

T. M. Murphy

Also by T.M. Murphy

The Belltown Mystery Series

The Secrets of Belltown
The Secrets of Cranberry Beach
The Secrets of Cain's Castle
The Secrets of Pilgrim Pond
The Secrets of Code Z
The Secrets of the Twisted Cross

The Running Waves
(with Seton Murphy)

Saving Santa's Seals

T.M. Murphy

Illustrations by Adam Taylor

A LeapKids Book
Leapfrog Press
Teaticket, Massachusetts

A LeapKids Book
Leapfrog Kids

Published in 2009 in the United States by
Leapfrog Press LLC
PO Box 2110
Teaticket, MA 02536
www.leapfrogpress.com

Printed in the United States of America

Distributed in the United States by
Consortium Book Sales and Distribution
St. Paul, Minnesota 55114
www.cbsd.com

First Edition

Library of Congress Cataloging-in-Publication Data

Murphy, Ted, 1969-
  Saving Santa's seals / T.M. Murphy ; illustrations
by Adam Taylor.
     p. cm.
  "A LeapKids Book."
  Summary: Eight-year-old Ryder's Christmas adventure
begins with a secret key, continues while he tries to
help his Uncle Ted overcome writer's block, involves
elves and captive seals, and ends with a very special
gift from Santa Claus.
  ISBN 978-0-9815148-8-8 (alk. paper)
  [1. Adventure and adventurers--Fiction. 2.
Christmas--Fiction. 3. Authorship--Fiction. 4.
Uncles--Fiction. 5. Seals (Animals)--Fictin. 6.
Elves--Fiction. 7. Santa Claus--Fiction.] I. Taylor,
Adam, ill. II. Title.
  PZ7.M9565Sav 2009
  [Fic]--dc22

     2009028921

For my parents, James F. Murphy Jr. and Margaret A. Murphy, for teaching me always to go for my dreams, even when the Coal Monsters try to block them!

Chapter 1

Wow! I guess there are hundreds and maybe even thousands of stories around the world that are about Christmas. Some are true stories. Some are not so true. And then there are the tales that lie in between truth and fantasy, confusing librarians about what category to give them and bookstore workers on what shelf to place them. These are the stories that are as magical as Christmas itself. They are meant for kids like me to make up our own minds about what we wish to truly believe.

For me, eight-year-old Ryder Matthews, it was those in-between Christmas stories that I always loved so much, but as I dreamt away on *that* snowy December morning, I had absolutely no clue that I was about to be the main character in one! Maybe the biggest unknown Christmas story yet!

But how could I know?

After all, I was too busy snoring away, probably

sounding like my grandpa during an afternoon nap and not a second grader about to wake up to chase after the school bus.

But on that magical day when *my* Christmas story, or better yet my Christmas *adventure* began, there was so much snow falling I wouldn't have to worry about over-sleeping.

But how could I have known that either?

I was still snoring away, probably now sounding more like a bear does right after eating ten jars of honey before hibernating for the winter.

I was hibernating alright! You see, I was beyond tired. The previous night, I had stayed up studying for my spelling test, and as a reward for my hard work, I got to talk on the phone with my uncle Ted.

Uncle Ted is a writer and he always tells me the coolest bedtime stories. You name it and he's told me about it. He has told me about knights who live in castles made out of dinosaur bones and about blue ghosts who eat bologna and cheese sandwiches, and once he even told me about a spaceman who landed on Mars and met aliens who rode around on French poodles.

Yup, Uncle Ted has told me the coolest stories, and I always looked forward to hearing a new one. But something strange happened when I talked to him the night before *my* Christmas adventure began.

"I'm sorry, Ryder, I'm really frustrated, I can't think of

any new stories," my uncle said sadly.

"But you always tell me new stories, Uncle Ted."

"I know, I'm sorry," he apologized.

"Well," I said, "could you please tell me one of your old stories?"

"OK," he replied. "How about the one about the sea captain?"

"Oh, yes, I love that one!"

For the next half hour, Uncle Ted told me the tale of Captain Salty Sam who was as mean and salty as a storm at sea until the day he discovered an entire island made out of chocolate. Then he became a lovable sweet tooth. That's how my uncle always told the story and I *always* loved it. Before I knew it, I was asleep dreaming of the milk chocolate lake where the captain caught red Swedish candy fish. I was probably still dreaming of it when my mom woke me up.

"Ryder, are you going to sleep the day away?"

I rubbed my eyes awake and looked at the alarm clock. "Oh no Mom! I'm going to be late for school! I'm going to miss my spelling test!"

"Ryder, I don't think there'll be a spelling test today." Dad came in and pointed at the window.

I poked my head up and my eyes bulged at the sight.

"Oh, wow! Mom and Dad! Look at all the snow! No school! No school! Yeah! Oh, wow! I want to build a snowman!" I pushed the covers off and started jumping up and down on my bed while my parents laughed.

"Yup, this *is* a perfect day to build a snowman! Enjoy your day off, Buddy. I have to go to work." Dad gave me a hug goodbye.

"I wish you could build a snowman with me, Dad."

"Me too, Buddy, but I'm looking forward to seeing one in the yard when I come home."

"OK, Dad! It will be my mission." I saluted Dad and he saluted back.

After breakfast, I put on my snowsuit and asked Mom the same question I had been asking her all morning.

"Mom, are you sure you don't want to build a snowman with me?"

"I wish I could, Ryder, but I have to watch your baby sister and she's too little to go outside."

"I understand, Mom. I'll build the best snowman right in front of the kitchen window so Baby Jenny can enjoy it. It will be my mission." I saluted again.

"That's a good brother." Mom kissed me on the cheek, zipped me up, and I was on my way out the door.

Now, you might think building a snowman isn't much of a Christmas adventure, but as I think back on how it all began, it really started the day I made that snowman. So please be patient and stay with me because this story gets pretty crazy!

Anyway, my dad was right. It *was* the perfect day to build a snowman, and I quickly got to work. First I made a snowball that I rolled and rolled until it became the huge bottom for the snowman's body. Then I rolled the middle and finally finished by making his head. After I gave him some small tree branches for arms, I knew what I had to do next.

"Alright, Mr. Snowman, it's time to give you a face." I patted him softly with my glove before going back into the house and opening the refrigerator door.

"Are you done already?" Mom asked while holding my little sister.

"No, Mom. I need to make Mr. Snowman's face. Do we have a carrot for his nose?"

"No, I was actually going to ask your dad to pick up some carrots and some milk on his way home from work."

"Aw, Mom. That will be too late. I need to make his face before Dad comes home."

"I'm sorry, Ryder, but you'll have to wait."

"Can *I* walk to the store and buy a nose for my snowman?"

Mom laughed. "Do you mean buy some carrots?"

"Yes. Please, Mom, please?"

"I'm sorry, but it's too far for you to walk. Maybe when you're older you can drive to the store by yourself."

"By then Mr. Snowman's face will be just one big old giant puddle," I said sadly.

Mom thought for a minute and then smiled. "I bet

if you go to Miss Haggerty's house and shovel her walkway she'll give you as many carrots as you want."

Miss Haggerty lived alone in a very old house just three houses away from us. Well, I shouldn't say she lived alone. She did have thirteen cats, six dogs, and a bird named Raven Ron. A few of the neighborhood kids were mean to Miss Haggerty and always called her "the Old Hag." I didn't know what that name meant but I knew it wasn't nice, so I just called her Miss Haggerty. But let's get something straight: that doesn't mean I didn't think Miss Haggerty wasn't a little creepy because she *was* creepy!

She would only come outside at night with Raven Ron perched on her shoulder while she walked her cats and dogs up the street. I have to tell you it was a weird sight to see thirteen cats on leashes and six dogs sniffing around leading Miss Haggerty up the street to who knows where. The other weird thing about her was that she only seemed to come out of her house just before Christmas time. I never saw her in the fall, spring, or summer!

Since it was the season, a couple of nights before I had seen her, so I had followed her home. I hid behind some bushes in her backyard and watched her pull out of her pockets what looked to be rocks. She then dumped them into a rusty old storage container. I was never able to get a look at what kind of rocks they were because Raven

Ron heard me and squawked at the bushes and then flew after me until I sprinted home for safety. Wow, talk about creepy!

So, now you know the reason I hesitated when Mom asked me to shovel Miss Haggerty's walkway.

"Ryder, Miss Haggerty doesn't have anyone else to help her and you do need a nose for your snowman." Mom pointed out the window at Mr. Snowman's blank face.

Yeah, but what if Raven Ron takes *my* nose, I thought, but then nodded. "OK Mom, I'll do it."

I grabbed my shovel and soon I was clearing a pretty good path to Miss Haggerty's old house. Well, I was until I felt an army of snowballs hit me in the back of the head. I turned around and saw three of the meanest fourth graders from my school. I didn't know their names. But I don't exactly ask people their names when they are knocking my books down, or pushing my face into a puddle, or in this case pelting me with snowballs.

"Why are you shoveling the Old Hag's place?" the biggest kid asked while he crouched down to scoop up more snow.

Even though I was a little scared, I said, "That's not her name. It's Miss Haggerty."

"Old Hag! Old Hag!" they all yelled together and fired more snowballs. I had nowhere to take cover, and I was in a bit of a daze. All I could hear was them laughing, and all I could feel were the snowballs exploding against my head. The mean kids did have good aim, I'll give them that. I was so scared that I didn't know what to do.

The front door suddenly opened and a hand waved to me, followed by a voice shouting, "Ryder, get in here! It's safe! Get in here, now!"

What was I going to do? It was either face the bullies or run into Miss Haggerty's house. When the ninth snowball hit me, I knew I didn't have any other choice, so I sprinted for the front door.

I slid into the house and Miss Haggerty shut the door behind me. When I looked around the dark house, I realized that the thirteen cats, six dogs, and Raven Ron were all staring at me.

"Hey second grader! I bet she's going to feed your eyes to her cats!" I heard the biggest kid yell from outside.

"Or she'll have that bird peck them out!" another kid added and they all laughed.

I had the same thought as I looked at Raven Ron's black eyes staring down at me. But then something strange happened. Miss Haggerty laughed and then she kept laughing, but not in a creepy way.

"What's so funny?" I asked.

She caught her breath and giggled. "It's just funny that bullies never change. They still say the same things that they were saying when I was a little girl. So Ryder, do you know how we get back at bullies like them?" She gave me a mischievous smile.

"No. How?"

"Like this." She opened the door and ordered to her animals, "Go get them!"

A second later, all the animals ran out the door. There were barks, meows, and squawks, but then came one of the best sounds ever. I peeked out and felt myself smiling when I saw where that sound was coming from.

One of the kids was shouting, "Oh, no! She let them loose!"

Another kid pointed. "They're coming for us!"

"Run! Run!" the biggest kid yelled in fright as all thirteen cats, six dogs, and even Raven Ron chased the bullies down the street.

When they were out of sight I turned to Miss Haggerty and we both burst into laughter. We continued to laugh and laughed even more when all of the animals came back into the house with their tongues dragging, even Raven Ron!

"That was *so* cool!" I said as Miss Haggerty led me into the sitting room where there was a warm wood fire.

"Yeah, it *was* pretty cool, wasn't it? So, Ryder, your mom called earlier and said you needed a carrot for the snowman you're building."

"Yes, Ma'am."

"Well, wait here, and I'll get one in the kitchen."

When Miss Haggerty left I realized something. She wasn't creepy at all, just a little different.

15

"Here you go." She handed me the best carrot nose ever.

"Aw, thanks," I said.

"No. Thank *you*, Ryder, for shoveling my walkway."

"No problem, Miss Haggerty. It turned out to be a lot of fun."

She smiled, walked over to her desk, sat down, and began writing in a big book.

"Ryder, what are their names?"

"Who?"

"The boys who were picking on you."

"I don't know."

She stopped writing and glanced up at me. "It's OK. I promise not to tell anyone you told me their names."

"Thanks, but that's not the reason. I really don't know their names. I just know they're really mean fourth graders."

"Oh." She put her pen away and shut the book.

"Miss Haggerty, why did you want to know their names, anyway?"

"Oh, it's nothing for you to worry about. I'm sure I'll find out who they are soon enough. I always do." She sighed.

"Well, I should get going," I said, but paused, looking at the front door, wondering if they were waiting down the road for me.

"If you're worried about those bullies, Ryder, you can

go out my back door and cut through the back yards to get home."

"Thanks. How did you know I might be worried?" I asked.

"Remember, I *was* little once. You see, everyone has to deal with mean people at some point in life; even those bullies will someday meet bigger bullies. But remember, Ryder, you can't *always* go out the back door. There will be a time when you'll have to face them just like you faced me, 'the Old Hag.'"

"What?"

"I know you were afraid of me."

"Well, maybe a little, but Miss Haggerty, you're not an old hag."

She laughed. "That's OK. In a way, the name those boys gave me was actually a compliment."

"Huh?" I was confused.

"You see, Ryder, it frightens them that I'm not like everyone else, so that's why they call me 'Old Hag.' But what they don't know is it's a lot safer in life to be like everyone else than to truly be who you are meant to be. But where is the fun in that? I'd rather be an original person. Being like everyone else, well, that's just boring."

"Well, you're certainly *not* boring and you're certainly *not* like everyone else, Miss Haggerty."

"Thanks but please call me Old Hag." She howled with laughter.

"OK, Old Hag." I smiled.

"Well, good luck on your long journey, Ryder Matthews." She nodded and shut the door behind me.

Long journey, I thought. Journey meant trip. It was hardly a long trip to my house. I stood there for a moment thinking of what an interesting character Miss Haggerty, the Old Hag, was. At least, that's how my uncle Ted would've described her, I thought as I stepped off the back stoop and was about to leave her backyard. But then I stopped when I noticed something. I was standing only a few feet away from the rusty old storage container. I always wondered why she had collected rocks at night, and what kind of rocks they were. Maybe they weren't even rocks. Maybe they were gold nuggets.

I bet it *is* gold, I thought. That's why she puts them there at night! It made sense, and now was my chance to find out.

I looked over my shoulder at the door and Miss Haggerty was nowhere in sight. Yup, I thought, I have to find out. I hustled over to the bin and took a deep breath before pulling the cover up. I expected to see pirate treasure rescued from a sunken ship or maybe even gold bars hidden from a bank robbery. But what I saw surprised me more than anything at all—coal.

Yes, hundreds and thousands of lumps of coal. I had no idea why Miss Haggerty had collected lumps of coal in the middle of the night, and why she would store it in an old, rusty container. I mean, nobody had a coal stove anymore! It made no sense.

What I did know was there was no way she needed all that coal, and I *did* need to make a face for my snowman. I figured Miss Haggerty wouldn't miss a few lumps so I grabbed six pieces and tucked them into my pockets. I walked home thinking of how my snowman would now have the perfect smile.

And I was right! After I used two buttons from my mom's sewing basket for eyes, branches for arms, the best carrot nose ever, and six pieces of coal for a wide smile, my dad announced it was the best snowman he had ever seen!

That night I tossed and turned but I couldn't sleep. Maybe it was because I had overslept that morning or maybe I was still excited from my day of building Mr. Snowman and meeting Miss Haggerty. Who knows?

Either way, I had run out of counting sheep and now I was counting pigs so I decided to go into the kitchen and get a glass of water. I turned on the outside light and then looked out the window to check on my snowman and couldn't believe it! Mr. Snowman's smile was glowing! Seriously, I mean glowing!

I almost dropped my glass. It made no sense. It looked like the coals were actually burning.

Maybe, I thought, my eyes are playing tricks on me. I knew what I had to do. I grabbed my red snowsuit and wiggled into it, almost tripping, and then ran outside.

"Oh, man! That's so cool!" I marveled at Mr. Snowman's glowing, red smile.

"It might look cool to you but it's not cool at all." The voice from behind startled me.

I turned around and there were Miss Haggerty's thirteen cats and six dogs all staring at me. Beside them stood Miss Haggerty with Raven Ron perched on her shoulder. This time she wasn't smiling or laughing, and neither were her animals.

"Ryder, why did you take my coal?"

"I . . . ah, ah, ah, I, didn't think you'd mind."

"You took the coal out of *my* bin," she stressed.

"Yes, but Miss Haggerty, there was so much coal and you don't even have a coal stove. I didn't think you'd miss it. I was going to give the coal back when my snowman melted."

"I see," she said, and it looked like she was thinking of what to say next. I know *I* sure didn't know what to say. I could barely speak!

"Well, Ryder, you should always ask people before borrowing something. Do you understand?"

"Yes, Ma'am." I nodded over and over.

"Good." Her smile returned and she walked over and one by one she took the lumps of coal off the snowman and placed them into her coat pocket.

When she was finished, she turned to me. "Ryder, you

now understand that this coal isn't meant for you or your snowman?"

"Yes, Miss Haggerty."

"I thought I told you to call me Old Hag."

"Oh, yes." I smiled. "Yes, Old Hag. Well, I should get back into the house. I'm really sorry Old Hag. I should've asked you for the coal."

"Yes, you should've, but I forgive you. I wasn't positive but now I know why I am here," she said.

"Huh?"

"Before you leave, Ryder, I have something for you." She reached into her pocket and handed me a necklace with a silver key attached to it. On the key was the letter *S*.

"What is this for?" I asked.

"This key necklace is for your secret journey. You can use it only once. So use it wisely."

"What secret journey?"

"It wouldn't be a secret if I told you, now would it?"

Miss Haggerty turned around and disappeared into the winter night with her thirteen cats, six dogs, and Raven Ron.

Yup, as I think back on it, I'm pretty sure that *was* the day my Christmas adventure began!

Chapter 2

I spent the next few days wondering why Miss Haggerty gave me the silver key on the necklace, and why I would need it for a secret journey. I had no idea what she meant and I was thinking of going to her house to ask her. I also spent those days in the playground running from the three bullies. They never caught me, but I knew they would eventually, so I finally gave up one day and picked indoor recess instead of playing outside with my friends. Let me tell you, it was no fun looking out the window watching my buddies having a good time while I was stuck inside helping my teacher clean the whiteboard. I knew what Miss Haggerty said was true. Someday I would have to face those bullies. I just wasn't ready. I guess I was too scared.

Christmas break finally came, and I knew that would buy me some time. Maybe after the long vacation they would forget all about me, I hoped. Probably not! But it was a good wish to have, and I was having it when I walked into my house and saw Mom sitting at the kitchen table.

Mom was hunched over blowing on her hot chocolate.

"Hey, Mom! Christmas break is here! I won't need this for a whole week!" I threw my backpack on a hook and sat across from her.

"Well, I think that calls for a celebration." She got up and poured me a hot chocolate and then asked, "Whipped cream or fluff, Sir?"

"I'm feeling like whipped cream today, Ma'am," I joked.

"Yes, whipped cream, a fine choice, Sir." She laughed and sprayed a good helping into my cup.

"Where's Baby Jenny?" I asked.

"Napping."

"Oh, she's usually up when I come home."

"I know. I let her sleep. I wanted to have some alone time with you today."

"OK, Mom. Is there something wrong?"

"Well, it's your Uncle Ted. . . ."

"Is he OK?" I rose from my chair.

"Yes. Yes. He's fine. It's just that he's very sad these days."

"I don't believe it. Uncle Ted is never sad. He's *always* happy."

"I know, Ryder, that's why I'm a little worried about him."

Suddenly, I had no desire to drink my hot chocolate.

"Well, why is he sad, Mom?"

"It seems Uncle Ted is suffering from writer's block."

I didn't know what writer's block was but it sounded terrible!

"Oh, no, writer's block!" I gasped. "Does that mean he's sick?"

"No, Honey, he's not sick," Mom said.

My mind was racing. "Oh, no! I knew it! I just knew it! It's worse than sick! I bet a big block fell on his head! Is that what happened, Mom? Did a big block fall on Uncle Ted's head?"

She laughed. "No, Honey, no big block fell on Uncle Ted's head and he can't get hurt from writer's block."

I was frustrated. "Well, then, what *is* writer's block, Mom?"

"Writer's block means Uncle Ted can't think up any stories to write."

"Do you mean he can't think up any *good* stories?"

Mom frowned. "I mean Uncle Ted can't think up *any* stories at all. I think he's forgotten why he loves to write for children. He needs something or someone to help him remember."

I thought for a minute and then said, "Mom, I think I can help him."

"You can? How?"

"Because he's been telling me stories ever since I was just a little baby. He taught me what makes up a good story because he told me once."

"He did? Well, what *does* make up a good story?" she asked.

"Uncle Ted said a good story is the type of tale that parents or uncles or aunts tell children at bedtime and when those children grow up to be parents or uncles or aunts they pass that story on. He said they wouldn't pass it on if it wasn't any good."

"Interesting." Mom nodded and took another sip of her hot chocolate.

"He said there is nothing more meaningful to the world than a good story," I added.

"Why is that?"

"Because it's a gift you leave for future boys and girls."

Mom smiled. "When I've let you stay up late to talk with Uncle Ted on the phone I never knew he was teaching you so much about storytelling."

"Oh, yeah." I got excited. "He also told me that as long as I was willing to dream maybe someday I'll find a good story, and if I do, I should never keep it to myself. You see, Mom, I know so much about this stuff. I know Uncle Ted needs my help."

Mom came over and hugged me. "I think he does,

Honey. So you wouldn't mind if Dad dropped you off at Uncle Ted's for the weekend?"

"Of course not, as long as I'm back for Christmas," I said.

"Of course. I'll call Dad and he can bring you to Uncle Ted's when he gets home from work."

"Sounds good, Mom. I'll help Uncle Ted get rid of his writer's block before Christmas. It will be my mission!" I saluted Mom and headed to my room to think of a plan.

I spent the afternoon trying to think up different stories that might help Uncle Ted, before packing and jumping into Dad's car.

"So Mom tells me you're going to try and cheer Uncle Ted up," Dad said after he backed out of our driveway, spun the wheel, and headed down the street.

"I sure hope so."

"That's a good boy. Mom and I were thinking about spending Christmas at Uncle Ted's house instead of our house this year. It might make him feel better. What do you think, Buddy?" He glanced over at me.

"But what about Santa?"

"What about Santa?" Dad repeated my question.

"Well, how will he know we're all at Uncle Ted's?"

Dad chuckled. "Don't worry about Santa. Santa will know. I don't know how the big guy does it but he'll know. It's just another one of the mysteries of Santa Claus."

"Really? Are you sure he'll know, Dad?"

"Yeah, I remember when I was a kid one Christmas and I had to go to my cousin's house in. . . ." Dad stopped talking and slowed down as we passed Miss Haggerty's house. There was a truck parked beside the house.

"Wow, they're already at it." Dad shook his head.

"Already at what?" I asked.

"Moving Miss Haggerty's stuff." He pointed to the lettering on the side of the truck that spelled *MERRY MOVERS*.

"I don't understand. Why is there a moving truck there?"

"Mom didn't tell you?"

"Tell me what?" I asked.

"Miss Haggerty is moving. Actually, she already left."

"She left? But, Dad, she's been living in that house for like . . . like . . . like. . . ."

"Like, forever, as you kids like to say," he filled in the sentence.

"Yeah, like forever."

"It might as well be forever. It's been over 50 years to be exact. It is very weird if you ask me. You know, Ryder, there was always something strange about her. It's no secret people only see her outside just before Christmas."

"I know." I nodded in agreement. "Did she say why she was leaving?"

"Yes. She said she couldn't work here anymore and

28

now her work has to be done elsewhere. That's also pretty strange considering the woman didn't work. All she really did was walk her animals."

"Yeah, pretty strange," I said softly.

"Hey, speaking of strange, wow, check those guys out!" Dad pointed.

Dad was right. It *was* strange. Beyond strange. There were about six of the shortest men I'd ever seen wearing identical red sweaters and matching hats. What was even weirder was that they were loading the rusty old storage container up into the back of the truck.

Why would anyone move that container of coal? I wondered.

I watched them and tried to figure out their height. They had to be only about three to five feet tall at the most.

Even though my Dad had the window up, it was almost as if the men had heard him talking because they all stopped, turned, and stared over at our car. Something made me feel like all their eyes were on me. After we passed, I looked over my shoulder and they had gone back to work.

"Ryder, those guys were kind of creepy, huh? I don't mean because they were short, but because they didn't look happy. They sure don't look like *Merry Movers* to me, but how can I blame them? Nobody wants to be working this close to Christmas."

"Yeah," I managed to say.

"It was strange though, Ryder, they were all looking at us like they knew us or something."

"Or knew me," I blurted.

"Huh? I didn't hear you." He moved his eyes off the road and onto me for a second.

"Oh, I was just agreeing with you, Dad. I was just saying that they *were* kind of creepy." I tried to sound like what I had just witnessed didn't bother me. But it did! I felt for my necklace tucked under my shirt and kept thinking of what Miss Haggerty had said to me—

This key necklace is for your secret journey.

As we drove that hour to my uncle's house, I couldn't help but wonder if *this* was the journey Miss Haggerty had been talking about. It wouldn't be long before I got my answer.

Chapter 3

During the rest of the ride, I tried to put Miss Haggerty and the *Merry Movers* out of my head and focus on my mission—to come up with a great story idea for Uncle Ted. I really hoped I could cure his writer's block, but then I got distracted thinking of the fun spot we were headed to.

Uncle Ted lived in a place called Cape Cod, and every time I visited there, he and I would do the coolest things. We would go scuba diving, or make sand castles at the beach, or go fishing, or play catch, or do my favorite thing in the world, which was ride around in *O'Nel's Ice Cream* truck.

Yes, Uncle Ted had a friend named O'Nel who owned an ice cream truck and lived next door to him. He told me the reason he and O'Nel were such good friends was because they both worked for children. Uncle Ted wrote kids' books, and O'Nel sold treats for kids. They always joked that *they* were actually the two biggest kids in town because they loved eating ice cream and telling stories.

Whenever I visited, I got to ride around in the truck with O'Nel and Uncle Ted to all the beaches and eat as much ice cream as I wanted! Wow, it was so cool!

But when Dad dropped me off at my uncle's house I realized that in the winter, Cape Cod was just like my town. There was snow everywhere!

Uncle Ted greeted me in the driveway. "Hey Ryder, you've only visited me in the summer, so what do you think of Cape Cod in the winter?"

"It's cold," I said, in shock.

"Yup. You can say that again."

"It's cold."

He gave a slight smile and grabbed my travel bag. "I'm sorry about it being cold. I guess that's why I was kind of surprised when your Mom called and said you wanted to visit me."

"Why would you be surprised?" I asked as we walked up the driveway and into his house.

"Well, because it's too cold to go scuba diving, or build sand castles, or go fishing, or do any of that kind of stuff we usually do."

I looked around Uncle Ted's house and noticed by his computer a barrel filled with crumpled up pieces of paper.

"That's OK, Uncle Ted. I'm not here to visit you for

those things. I've come here for a more important reason."

"A more important reason? What is that?"

"I'm here to help you."

"Help me?" he asked, looking puzzled.

"Yes. I'm here to help you get rid of that awful old writer's block," I said confidently.

Uncle Ted smiled a bit. "Oh, really. You heard about that. And how will you help me?"

We walked into his living room and sat down on the couch.

"Well, I was thinking of some stories you could write."

"OK, Ryder, I'm all ears."

"Well, you should write a story about a seagull that rides a bicycle and eats *licorice*."

Uncle Ted scratched his head and said, "Umm. . . . That's sounds a little *ridiculous*."

"Then you should write about an alligator with a big, blue *toe*."

He shook his head and laughed. "Um, *no*. I don't think *so*."

I was desperate. "How about a story about a dog that wears a bow tie and speaks *Japanese*?"

"Oh, Ryder, my little nephew, *please*, oh, *please!*"

"I'm sorry, Uncle Ted, I just wanted to help you out." I shrugged, sadly.

"Oh, Ryder, I'm the one who should be sorry. I'm just so frustrated. It's certainly not your fault I can't think up any good stories. Please forgive me, I didn't mean to snap at you."

"That's OK. I understand. There is one good thing, Uncle Ted."

"What's that?" he asked.

"Well, we just rhymed like they do in some picture books."

He laughed and it was good to hear him laugh. "We did rhyme, didn't we?"

"Yup."

"Maybe, Ryder, you can help me come up with an idea if we just forget about stories and have some fun. So what do you want to do?"

I looked around his house and noticed something was different from my house.

"Uncle Ted, you don't have any Christmas decorations, and where is your tree?"

"I decided it was too much work to get one this year."

"Too much work?" I smiled. "No wonder you can't think up any good stories. You need a Christmas tree."

"I don't understand." He shrugged. "What does that have to do with my writer's block?"

"Remember when I asked you why you can write for children?"

35

"Yes," Uncle Ted answered and added, "And I said I can write for children because I can think like them."

"Well, if you don't have a Christmas tree how can you think like a child? And how is Santa going to come here?"

"Santa?" he asked me.

"Yeah, Mom and Dad said we might spend Christmas here."

"Really?"

"Yeah, to cheer you up. But how is Santa going to even know this is a Christmas house if there's no tree? Geeze, you might have the Easter Bunny visit instead. You need a tree."

Uncle Ted laughed. "You know what, you are so right, my little nephew. It might really help me and it will definitely help Santa when he puts your toys under the tree."

I nodded, smiled, and raced for the door. "So let's go get one."

"OK, OK. Wait up," he said as I hustled outside and then saw one of the best sights ever—O'Nel's ice cream truck parked next door. The truck was always painted green, yellow, and red but this time I noticed something different about it. There were white Christmas lights decorating it.

Most ice cream trucks played music that sounded like music from a carnival, but not O'Nel's. He was from Jamaica and he always played Reggae music while he drove his truck around the beaches. His music was always warm and happy.

So even though it was freezing cold I heard the happy-sounding music playing and it warmed me right up!

"O'Nel, what are you doing to your truck?" Uncle Ted asked when we saw O'Nel standing on a ladder holding another string of white lights.

"I'm decorating her," he said.

"I don't understand. I thought you put your truck away in the winter?" Uncle Ted replied.

"I normally do, but I woke up this morning and I felt there was magic in the air. So I decorated my truck and stored it with some ice cream, or as I like to call it, 'Nice cream.'"

"Magic?" I asked.

O'Nel laughed when he spotted me. "Oh, the little Ryder man is here. Then there really is magic blowing around in that winter wind. I just knew it. We have to see where the magic takes us. Don't you agree, little Ryder?"

"I sure do, O'Nel."

"Well then, help me finish decorating the truck with these happy lights and we'll take a journey. I bet something special is waiting for us."

When I heard the word *journey* I ran over and grabbed the string of lights. Uncle Ted didn't move as quickly.

"O'Nel, are you crazy? There's *no* magic in this wind or any other wind." My uncle shook his head.

O'Nel looked at me. "What's wrong with your uncle? He usually believes in magic more than me."

I whispered back, "He has writer's block."

O'Nel nodded. "I understand now. We have to let these lights take him somewhere special then. I knew there was a reason I was doing this."

"Your ice cream truck with the happy lights is not going to take me anywhere special," Uncle Ted laughed.

"That's not true," I interrupted.

"What do you mean, little Ryder man?" O'Nel looked down at me.

"You could take us to get a Christmas tree. Uncle Ted needs one. Wouldn't that be special?" I asked.

O'Nel looked at Uncle Ted and then smiled at me. "Yes, of course he needs one. You are so right. Everyone hop on board."

We jumped on O'Nel's truck and as we drove along I just knew O'Nel was right; something special was waiting for us. I just didn't know how special it would be!

Chapter 4

There may have been a foot of snow on the ground, but riding in O'Nel's truck sure made it feel like summer. I realized I wasn't the only one who felt that way when I spotted a group of kids sledding. They suddenly stopped and began chasing after us, yelling, "Stop the truck! Stop the truck! Please O'Nel, we want some ice cream!"

O'Nel looked back at Uncle Ted and me and said, "I'm sorry, the Christmas tree will have to wait. I can't say no to the kids."

"That's OK," Uncle Ted and I replied.

O'Nel pulled the truck over and the group of four kids huddled up to the counter.

"Even though your lips are blue, you all still want the ice cream?" he asked, smiling at the kids.

"Yes! Please, O'Nel! Please!" they chanted as they searched their pockets for their money, but then their excitement died and they all began whispering to one another.

"Let me guess, you kids don't have any money," O'Nel said.

"No, we didn't think we'd need any money if we were just sledding. We didn't expect to see *you*," one of the kids answered for the group.

O'Nel turned to me and said, "Little Ryder man, open that cooler and get me four ice cream bars for the kids."

"But they just said they have no money," I pointed out to him.

"If I say no to good children at Christmas time Santa will be pretty upset with me. I don't want to end up on his naughty list." He laughed, took the bars from me and passed them to the kids.

One by one they ripped open the ice cream wrappers while thanking him.

"Thanks so much, O'Nel!"

"You're the best!"

"Yeah, thank you and Merry Christmas!"

"Yeah, I hope Santa's good to you this year!"

"I hope so too." O'Nel chuckled as he started the truck, and the kids waved goodbye while we headed down the road for the Christmas tree farm.

"O'Nel, what do *you* want for Christmas?" Uncle Ted asked him.

"I don't want anything for myself Ted, but I do want something for some other people. Maybe, if I ever get the chance to talk to Santa I can tell him what that is."

"So, you aren't going to tell us?" I asked.

"Nope."

"Well, at least tell us who the some other people are," Uncle Ted said.

"Ted, unless you grow a beard and a big belly and drive a sleigh, I'm going to keep my Christmas wish to myself." O'Nel smiled and pointed ahead. "Here we are at the Christmas tree farm."

He pulled the door crank and the doors swished open. The three of us hopped down the steps, but as we walked into the farm I noticed a truck with lettering on its side—*MERRY MOVERS*—drive by slowly. The short driver was wearing a red sweater. He slowed almost to a stop and stared at me a long time before finally speeding up and continuing down the road.

"That's impossible. It couldn't be," I said softly, thinking there was no way it could be the same truck from Miss Haggerty's house. After all, Uncle Ted lived an hour away from me.

Maybe, I wondered, the company hires only people who look alike. Yeah, that must be it. But why would they do that? That made no sense. And why did the worker give me the same long stare the other workers had given me?

I didn't understand what I had seen *and* I didn't like it, but my mind quickly focused on why I was walking in the woods surrounded by trees of all sizes.

"Ryder, which one should I get?" Uncle Ted said, holding an ax the owner of the farm had just given him.

"I don't know. There are so many to choose from. Which one do you like, Uncle Ted?"

"I don't know. It's no big deal. They all look alike to me."

"Nonsense, Ted." O'Nel shook his head. "The trees all have their own personalities. There's the fat ones, the skinny ones, the tall ones and the small ones. You have to pick the one that will give you the best Christmas memory. After all, we *are* taking the tree from its family."

"Geeze, now that you put it that way, I don't know if I even want a tree," Uncle Ted said.

"No, you shouldn't feel bad because all of these trees have dreamt about this day."

"This day?" I asked O'Nel.

"Yes, the day they will be dressed up with care and become a Christmas tree. But your Uncle Ted has to pick the best one for *him*."

"O'Nel," my uncle interrupted, "you mean pick the best one for *all* of us." And then he smiled.

"Yes, for all of us," I agreed.

"So, that means we should split up and pick out our favorite tree and then we will decide as a team," Uncle Ted suggested.

"Sounds like a plan," O'Nel agreed.

We all went in different directions and pretty soon I was inspecting each tree, wondering if it was the perfect one for my uncle's house. I didn't exactly know what I was really looking for, but that didn't stop me from walking through an endless maze of trees. After a while, I realized that the longer I walked, the bigger the trees got and the darker the day became.

"Ryder, where are you?" I heard my uncle yell in the distance.

I cupped my hands and yelled back, "I'm over here!"

"Where?" Uncle Ted's voice sounded really far away.

I looked around and didn't know what else to say but "over here!"

"I can't find you." His voice faded in the wind.

I felt a chill go up my spine and it wasn't from the cold weather! I realized I was lost, and suddenly I was really scared. I heard a rustling noise coming from behind a row of trees.

"Uncle Ted, is that you?" I asked, hopeful.

There was no response; but then I heard the rustling again.

"O'Nel, *please*, say it's you."

After I said that, it became quiet, then the wind picked up and the rustling noise returned; but this time it was followed by the sound of jingling bells.

No, it couldn't be, I thought, but then I asked the

question anyway, "Santa, is that you?" There was no answer, just the sound of jingling bells. Even though I was still a little nervous, I walked over to the row of trees, crouched down and slowly pushed the branches aside. I had no idea what I was about to see when I ducked my head in between the trees.

"Agggh!" I yelled at the two eyes staring back at me.

"Agggh!" I yelled even louder when I realized those eyes belonged to the small man with the black beard! I noticed there were little bells attached to his *Merry Movers* uniform.

"Give me that!" He growled while his hands lunged and grabbed for my neck.

"Agggh," was still the only word that came out of my mouth.

"Give me that!" he demanded.

"Give you what?!" I finally managed to say as I backed away.

"The key necklace! Give it to me now!" he ordered while his hands grabbed again for my necklace.

"No! Get away from me!" I screamed and pushed him to the ground.

I have to get out of here, I thought, and turned and ran like my pants were on fire.

"Come back! Come back!" the mover hollered as he chased me through the maze of trees.

"Why?!" I shouted over my shoulder.

As I turned the corner to go down another row of trees, I heard him reply with a shout, "You have to give me that key or Christmas could be ruined!"

That stopped me dead in my tracks. What was this crazy little man talking about? I was too curious. I had to find out. I turned around but the man was so far behind me that he still hadn't turned the corner.

"What do you mean Christmas could be ruined?" I yelled, hearing his bells approaching the corner.

"Christmas could be ruined? Christmas *won't* be ruined." I heard another voice from behind me. It was Uncle Ted. He and O'Nel were carrying a beautiful green tree. I moved my eyes from them back to the corner, expecting the little man to come around it, but he didn't. Then I realized I could no longer hear the jingling bells.

"We *were* going to ask your opinion on which tree to pick, Ryder, but we couldn't find you. What have you been doing all this time?"

I was a half-second away from telling Uncle Ted about the Merry Mover chasing me when I again remembered what Miss Haggerty had said to me—*This key necklace is for your secret journey.*

How could I take a secret journey if I told people? I had to keep it to myself. At least for now, I decided. The other question that stayed with me as we tied the tree to the truck was, why would my having the key necklace ruin *Christmas?*

I had no idea how I was going to find the answer to that question. Little did I know the answer was actually going to find me!

Chapter 5

My mind was still spinning with questions as we drove through the center of town and then along the street that overlooked the harbor. Out of nowhere, those questions suddenly were replaced with voices.

"Help! Help us! Please!"

Oh, no, voices in my head, I thought, I must *really* be losing my mind!

But then I heard them again.

"Please! Help us! Please, little boy, help us!"

I rubbed the back window with my glove, stared through, and realized the voices weren't in my head at all. They were coming from near the aquarium we had just passed.

"Stop the truck! Stop the truck!" I hollered.

O'Nel slammed on the brakes. "What's wrong, little Ryder man?"

"Don't you guys hear that?" I asked.

O'Nel and Uncle Ted looked at one another and then turned to me. "Hear what?"

I pointed my finger toward the aquarium and waited for the voices, but this time it was silent.

"I swear that just a minute ago, I heard some people calling for help."

"You must be mistaken, little Ryder man. No one would be out in this cold by the aquarium. After all, it's closed for the winter," O'Nel explained.

"I'm telling you I heard some people. They sounded like they were in trouble. We have to check it out," I pleaded.

O'Nel laughed. "It was probably that magical winter wind I was talking about earlier. It's now blowing around playing tricks with your imagination."

"I'm telling you it wasn't my imagination! Guys, we have to check it out!" This time I demanded.

O'Nel chuckled again and was about to pull back onto the road when Uncle Ted came to my rescue. "O'Nel, it wouldn't hurt to take a look just to be safe."

"But Ted, you heard what I just said. The aquarium is closed."

"Yes, I know. But you know Ryder. If we don't take a look, he'll be talking about it all night," Uncle Ted said and turned to me. "Am I right, Ryder?"

"Yup." I nodded and folded my arms.

"Alright, if it will ease the little Ryder man's mind,

but then I want to get home to a warm fire." O'Nel gave in and we all got out of the ice cream truck and headed toward the aquarium.

After we looked around for a moment O'Nel pointed. "See. There's no one out here except those two Arctic Ice Seals and they're taking a snooze."

"Yeah, they might be in a caged tank but they sure don't look like prisoners to me." Uncle Ted laughed. "They're sound asleep. I bet they get fed pretty well since they're sleeping away looking like me after Christmas dinner."

"I guess you're right and I was wrong. There's nobody here who needs our help," I confessed. "But, O'Nel, how do you know these are Arctic Ice Seals?"

"The sign." O'Nel pointed and read it to us. "*These Arctic Ice Seals are new to the aquarium. Their names are Gus and Jack.*"

Suddenly, a loud banging noise came from behind the aquarium.

"What was that?" Uncle Ted asked.

"I don't know but we should take a look," O'Nel suggested.

Uncle Ted turned to me. "Ryder, why don't you stay here by the seal tank. We'll be right back."

Before I could object O'Nel and Uncle Ted walked behind the building. I was a little nervous, so I said to the tank, "Gus and Jack, I wish you'd wake up so I'd at least have some company."

To my surprise, the seals did just that. But to my absolute shock something else then happened.

"We weren't really sleeping and our names *aren't* Gus and Jack," one of the seals said in a perfect-sounding *human* male voice.

"What?" I gasped.

"Yes," the other seal added. "I mean, little boy, do I really look like a 'Gus' to you? I am a lady, a lady of royalty, no less."

"Huh?" My eyes almost popped out of my head. The second seal spoke in a sweet *female* voice!

"He can hear us. That means the little boy is a good one, Zandra," the seal with the male voice said, and they both nodded to one another.

I put my hands over my eyes. "Okay, I must be losing my mind completely! What am I going to do?"

"You're not losing your mind, little boy. You *can* hear us because we *are* speaking. That was us yelling for help a minute ago," the female said.

"This can't be happening." I kept my hands over my face, hoping everything would go back to normal, but it didn't.

"Please take your hands off your eyes. We don't have much time. We really *do* need your help," the female said to me.

I reluctantly took my hands away. "I can't believe I'm

going to say this but how can you talk? I mean you're seals for crying out loud!"

"Well, we're not just any seals," the female continued. "We're *Santa's Seals*."

"Huh?"

The female waddled forward. "First off, we heard your uncle say your name. It's Ryder, right?"

"Ye . . . s," my mouth barely managed.

"So, allow us to introduce ourselves. My name is Zandra. I am a fourth-generation Santa Seal. I am named after the beautiful seal Queen Zandra who ruled *Zandraland* with a kind heart and a merry soul. Someday I hope to do the same."

"*Zandraland?*"

"Yes, the land of magical seals. Queen Zandra was the first seal to discover the *Christmas Caves*."

"*Christmas Caves?*" I asked.

"The caves that help Santa Claus. Wow, so much to tell you. We'll get to the *Christmas Caves* in a minute," she said and gestured with her left fin. "And this is my new partner Bob. This will be his first Christmas swimming through the caves. That is, if we can get out of here."

The other seal moved forward and placed his fin against the chain-linked cage. "Nice to meet you, Ryder."

"Nice to meet you, too, Bob. So, if Zandra is named after the Seal Queen who ruled with a merry heart and a kind soul, who are you named after?" I asked.

"A guy named Bob who ruled a fish market with a merry heart and free salmon on Fridays."

Zandra lifted her head and laughed.

"My parents first met in a harbor under the dock next to Bob's Fish Market, so Bob I am," he added.

"Oh, Bob, you are so funny!"

"I am?" He turned to Zandra and she laughed again but then stopped.

"I wish we could laugh all night but we don't have time. We need your help, Ryder. We were captured, and we need to get back to Santa before Christmas."

"My help? How can *I* help two talking seals? I'm just a kid. No one would ever believe me."

"You're right," she said, "most adults wouldn't believe you because only good children can understand us when we speak. Adults don't hear our words at all. They just hear the barks of seals."

"That's true with bad children, too. We sound like regular seals to them. That's why we know you're a good child, Ryder. You understand us," Bob added.

"That's it." Zandra slapped her fins together. "I've got an idea. Maybe, if you got some good children together you could all think up a plan and free us."

"That's a great idea, Zandra," I said, "but the problem is I'm visiting my uncle, so I don't know any children in this town." But then I stopped talking when I felt a tap on my shoulder. I turned around and a tall man hovered over me.

"Who are you talking to, little boy?" The man stared down at me and then glanced over at Zandra and Bob.

"Oh, no, it's him!" Zandra gasped.

"I said, who are you talking to, little boy?" the man repeated.

"No one, Sir. I was ah . . . talking to myself."

"You can understand those seals can't you?" he asked with a snarly smile.

"Ryder, please don't answer him! He is very dangerous. He is the man who caught us. He knows about the *Christmas Caves!* He wants what's in them! If he finds out you understand us, he'll kidnap you!" Zandra pleaded.

"Why would he kidnap mmm. . . ." I blurted to Zandra and the tall man's snarl grew wider.

"Oh, I knew it." The man rubbed his hands. "This whole thing will be even easier than I thought."

The man lunged forward to grab me but then O'Nel and Uncle Ted suddenly appeared from behind the building.

Uncle Ted thumbed over his shoulder. "That noise was just an open door blowing in O'Nel's magical wind."

The tall man's snarl instantly turned to a frown when he spotted Uncle Ted and O'Nel and he moved away from me.

"Hello," Uncle Ted said.

"Hello. I'm sorry but we are closed for the winter," the tall man replied.

"Oh, you run the aquarium?" Uncle Ted asked.

"Yes, I just bought it last month."

"Well, you have a broken door in the back," O'Nel said.

"Oh, thank you. I'll have to check that out."

"Well, since you're new to our town we should introduce ourselves. My name is Ted and this is O'Nel and it seems you've met my nephew, Ryder."

"Yes, what a good little boy he is." The tall man smiled at me and I knew it was a fake smile!

"And your name is?" Uncle Ted asked.

"Dr. Gloomsday."

"Gloomsday," Uncle Ted and O'Nel both repeated.

"Yes, I know. It's a rather unfortunate name. But we can't always choose our names, can we?"

"You're a doctor?" I asked in shock.

"Yes, I am a doctor of the ocean. I know everything about the ocean. I know things other people wouldn't believe even if they saw them with their own two eyes." He flashed his fake smile at me and I almost couldn't move. I wanted to tell Uncle Ted and O'Nel but there was no way they would believe me. *I* almost didn't believe it, so how could they?

"Well, we should get going," O'Nel said.

"Yeah, we woke the poor seals up from their nap." Uncle Ted pointed. Then he said to me, "OK Ryder, time to go put up the Christmas tree."

O'Nel hopped into the truck and Uncle Ted followed. I was still staring at Zandra and Bob, thinking of how I could save them, but then my eyes met those of the evil Dr. Gloomsday.

"Until we meet again, Ryder," he whispered.

His words made me race to the truck, but then I heard Zandra's voice in the distance.

"Please, Ryder, please come back and rescue us!" she yelled in desperation.

I turned around, saluted and silently said, "Yes, Zandra and Bob. I will come back. It will be my mission, Zandra. Yes, it will be my secret mission."

As O'Nel drove away, Uncle Ted gave me a long, strange look and said, "Ryder, when you were outside did you just. . . ?"

But then he stopped talking.

"Did I just what, Uncle Ted?"

"Never mind. It's nothing," he said.

It *was* something, but I wouldn't know until much later what exactly that *something* was!

Chapter 6

That night I was pretty quiet while Uncle Ted put on Christmas music and we decorated the tree. He hummed away and he seemed to be getting into the holiday spirit, but there was no way that *I* could enjoy the moment. I was too busy trying to make sense of all the crazy events of the day. I still had a thousand unanswered questions jumbling around in my brain. Some were old ones. Why would the Merry Mover chase me around asking for the key necklace? And why would *my* having the key necklace ruin Christmas? Some were new ones. Could there really be talking seals? Maybe it was my imagination playing tricks on me. But if it wasn't, were they *really* Santa's Seals? And what was in those Christmas Caves that Dr. Gloomsday wanted so much? Whatever it was, it had caused him to trap the seals and almost kidnap me!

It was that last thought that I couldn't shake, and that

also had *me* shaking, as Uncle Ted tucked me into bed.

"So, Ryder, you don't seem yourself tonight. You seem like you're not completely here, like you're in another land or something. Is everything alright?"

Yeah, I'm in *Zandraland*, I wanted to say, but instead answered, "Yeah, Uncle Ted. I'm fine."

"Well, Ryder, you know if there is something bothering you, you can tell me."

"I know Uncle Ted, but really, I'm fine. I'm just really tired." I faked a yawn.

"OK, Buddy. Well, I wish I could tell you a bedtime story but it seems I still have writer's block. By the way, did you come up with any good story ideas today?"

Even though I was still nervous about the Merry Mover and Dr. Gloomsday, I had to laugh at my uncle's question. Oh, I had come up with a good idea for a story, alright, but it was a story idea that might put the seals in even more danger if I told someone. Plus the fact that it was a *true* story that no one would ever believe! I still wasn't sure if I did.

"What's so funny?" my uncle asked.

"I was just thinking again of my idea about the dog that wears a bow tie and speaks Japanese."

"Oh, that one, yes, maybe we can talk about that idea in the morning. Kids *do* love make-believe stories about talking animals. Well, goodnight, Buddy." Uncle Ted switched the light off and shut the door.

"Well, they might also love a story about two seals who can talk, but there's nothing make-believe about Zandra and Bob. At least, I don't think so," I whispered softly to myself. Then I heard the sound of jingling bells. I knew that sound. I had heard that jingling only a few hours earlier—the Merry Mover!

He was in the room! I peeked over my covers and saw the moon's reflection on the open closet door. Normally, I would've thought it was a coat or shirt hanging making it look like a clothes monster, but I knew better when I heard the jingling bells. I pulled the covers over my face and froze.

What am I going to do?

The jingling bells moved closer to my bed, and I tried to pull the covers even higher over me, but I knew there was no escaping him.

"Please don't hurt me," I begged with a whisper.

There was no response and the silence was worse than anything, but then a light flashed in my eyes.

"Aggh!" I screamed.

"Sshh!" the Merry Mover said, waving the flashlight in his hand. "Keep it down. Your uncle might hear you!"

"Well, isn't that the point?!" I heard myself shout.

"I'm not going to hurt you. I just came here for the key."

"Why should I give you that?"

"Because *Santa* needs it."

"Santa? I don't understand."

"It's a long story." He reached forward, but I pushed him away and he fell to the floor.

"Cheese and crackers kid, why do you have to be so difficult?" he asked as he jingled back to his feet.

"My *name* is Ryder and you're telling me *I'm* difficult? What about you? Who do you think *you* are to come in here and take my necklace?" Now I was more angry than scared.

"I'm doing this for Santa Claus," he said. "If he doesn't get that key Christmas could be ruined."

"Yeah, yeah, I know, you said that when you chased me around the Christmas tree farm. But I don't believe you. You probably don't even know Santa."

"Of course I do."

"How?" I asked.

"I work for him."

"What do you mean you work for him?" I was puzzled.

"I *mean* I'm one of Santa's Elves."

That *would* explain why he was so short, I thought, but that didn't mean I believed him.

"OK, what's your name then?"

"My name is Jay the Elf. Look Ryder, I really don't have time for all of your questions."

"Jay the Elf," I repeated. "Wait, I don't believe you. You can't be an elf."

"What do you mean you don't believe I'm an elf? Take a good look at me. I'm a grown man who is three feet nine inches tall wearing a red uniform with bells attached to it. If I'm not an elf then the tooth fairy isn't a tooth!"

"Huh?"

"I mean the tooth fairy isn't a fairy! Cheese and crackers, Ryder, you got me all frazzled!"

"Yeah, but elves should have names like Eddie the Elf, or Edger the Elf, or Ernie the Elf, or. . . ." I was trying to think of other names when he jumped in and added to the list, "Yeah or Earl, Eliot, and Edwin the Elf. Yeah, *I* know them all and they're all good guys. But there are plenty of elves who don't have names that start with 'E' and I'm one of those elves, Jay the Elf."

I still wasn't sure if I believed him so I said, "I need to see some proof."

"Oh, cheese and crackers with extra cheese, you really *are* difficult," he said and reached into his pocket, pulled out his wallet, and handed it to me.

I opened it up and found a card with his picture on it. I read it out loud.

"This Learner's Permit To Drive Santa's Sleigh Is For Jay—A Second Year Santa Elf-In-Training." I looked up at him. "Wow, I can't believe it!"

"OK," Jay said, "So, I'm not exactly an elf yet, but I am going to be one if everything goes well this Christmas, and it *was* until you ended up with that key."

"Oh," I said and felt the key around my neck.

"Now if I don't hurry, I might never become a real elf. Aw, cheese and crackers with jelly beans, I should've known that I'd be no good at this elf stuff. I'm a complete failure." Jay sat down on the foot of my bed and buried his face in his hands.

I pushed the covers off, got out of bed, walked over, and patted him on the shoulder. "I'm sorry. I didn't mean to make you cry."

"That's OK, Ryder, it's not *your* fault. I'm the one who sent Miss Haggerty the wrong key. I really should just quit."

"You can't quit."

"Why not?"

"Because if you're crying, Jay, that means you really want to be an elf. Just think, you'll be crying even more if you stop trying to *become* an elf."

Jay looked up and wiped his eyes dry. "Now I understand why Miss Haggerty thought you were such a good little boy."

"Thanks. But why *would* you give a key to Miss Haggerty?"

"A few days ago, Santa asked me to send Miss Haggerty a new key for the coal bin because her old one broke. That's why the bin wasn't locked when you went to her house—because I grabbed the wrong key off Santa's desk and sent it to her. Obviously, that's also why I'm here without the other elves. They have no idea of my mistake."

"I'm confused. Why would you be sending Miss Haggerty a key to that old coal bin?"

"Well, since I told you so much already, I might as well keep going. The truth is Miss Haggerty also works for Santa."

"What?"

"Yup. Santa told me she has a high-level position in his *Naughty or Nice Division*."

"*Naughty or Nice Division*? What is that?"

"Her job is to find out which children have been nice and which have been naughty. She keeps a list and yes, Santa does check it twice."

"What? You're kidding?" I was amazed.

"It's no joke. That's why she had to move out of your town because you saw the coal bin—and imagine what would happen if you told someone."

"What would happen?"

"Other kids would find out and she wouldn't be able to do her job right. You see, Santa has people all over the world who collect names for the *Naughty or Nice* list. They also collect the coal for those names and they are in charge of putting that coal in the bad children's stockings on Christmas Eve."

"I always thought that was Santa's job," I said.

"It was but he hated it. Think about it, Ryder. He's

Jolly Old St. Nick. The man hates to punish children, but he also knows that if bad children don't get coal in their stockings, it will be very unfair to the *good* little boys and girls. So, many years back Santa hired a person in every town in every part of the world to keep the list and also pass out the coal for him."

"Why did he pick Miss Haggerty?"

"Santa always picks someone who is a little different from everyone else because those people are able to truly find out which girls and boys are really naughty, and which ones are really nice and not just pretending so they can get gifts. For example, Miss Haggerty wrote in her *Naughty or Nice* book that you'll be on the nice list every year but the bullies who threw the snowballs at you. . . . Well . . . they're going straight to the naughty list."

"Wow, that's pretty amazing. But I still don't understand why *my* having *this* key could ruin Christmas?"

"Well, the key I sent to Miss Haggerty by mistake is a very magical key and it can only be used once. It can unlock anything in the world, even Santa's Secret Toy Room. Imagine if it got into the wrong hands. The future of Christmas could be ruined."

"What is Santa's Secret Toy Room?"

"It's the room where Santa Claus comes up with all his new toy ideas. He has cabinets and cabinets of future toys that he will show us elves how to make someday, but he only takes the ideas out of the room when they are absolutely ready to be made. No one is allowed in that room, not even the elves, even though someday we'll be building those toys."

"So this key can open that room?"

"A magical Santa key can open really any room in the world. That's why it's so valuable. Santa has thousands of magical Santa keys made up every year."

"Why thousands?"

"Because he can't always make it down the chimney, so when that happens he uses one of the magical keys. After it is used once, the key becomes worthless."

"If he can make magic keys, wouldn't it be easier for Santa to make just one key that could open all houses and places he needs to go?"

"He used to have just one key that opened every place in the world but then one Christmas about 30 years ago, he left it at a house by mistake. Santa and his reindeer had flown all the way to New York City before he realized he left it by a plate of cookies in a house in Italy. That year he almost wasn't able to get all the presents out in time, so now he carries a key ring with thousands of magical keys on it. I just don't understand why *this* key wasn't on the ring."

"Yeah, that's strange, but *now* I understand why there is an 'S' on the key. 'S' is for Santa Claus. I always thought the S stood for secret," I said.

"What would make you think that?"

"Because Miss Haggerty said I would need this key for my secret journey."

"She told you that?" Jay squinted.

"Yup. Why do you think she said that?"

"Ryder, I have no idea what Miss Haggerty meant by that and I still don't know why she would give you, a little boy, such an important key. I've never met her, but I heard she's usually very good at her job." Jay stood up and paced back and forth.

I also had no idea why she would give me the key, but then a thought smacked me in the head like a baseball.

"The locked cage!"

"What?" He looked at me.

I grinned. "I don't know *how* Miss Haggerty knew it but I *do* know why she gave me this key. She *did* have a very good reason."

"Well, what is it, Ryder?"

"Jay, you said this key can open anything, right?"

"Yes, why?"

"I think, Jay the Elf, you and I were meant to meet for a reason."

"What reason is that?"

"To team up and save Santa's Seals."

Jay's eyes widened. "Santa's Seals! Wait! How do you know Santa has seals? Only people who work for Santa know about them. And what do you mean we have to *save* them? Tell me!"

"It's a long story, but Zandra and Bob need us." I hurried to my drawer.

"What?! How do you know about Zandra and Bob?"

"I'll tell you on the way there, but we have to get going on our secret journey," I said, putting my jeans on over my pajama pants.

"I'm so confused! What secret journey?" Jay asked.

"Well, the secret journey to save Christmas, of course! It's our mission!" I saluted Jay, not realizing what an amazing journey was ahead of us!

Chapter 7

Before we left Uncle Ted's house, I spent the next five minutes telling Jay the Elf all about Dr. Gloomsday capturing Zandra and Bob and how the evil doctor had tried to kidnap me. When I finished the story, Jay again demanded that I hand over the key, saying, "This is way too dangerous a job for a little boy."

In my mind I agreed with him, but what was also in my mind was the fact that I had given my word to Zandra that I would rescue her and Bob. There was no way I was going to let her down so I replied, "I'm not taking this key off my neck until we're at the aquarium and I'm unlocking that gate."

At first Jay the Elf was pretty upset with me, but he finally gave up when he realized I wasn't going to give in

"I still have a few unanswered questions," I said to him as he drove us to the aquarium.

Jay looked over at me and shrugged. "Well, you

might as well ask them, Ryder. There's no sense in me keeping anything secret from you anymore, since we have to work as a team now to save Zandra and Bob."

"OK. One, what exactly is the kind of work the seals do for Santa? Two, what are the *Christmas Caves*? And three, what is so valuable in those caves that made Dr. Gloomsday kidnap Zandra and Bob?"

"Cheese and crackers with a pepperoni stick," Jay sighed. "You do ask all the tough questions, don't you?"

I just nodded for him to continue.

"OK, this is one of the biggest secrets of Christmas, and few people have heard it before, but here it goes. You see, there are thousands and thousands of seals from *Zandraland* who work for Santa. Every Christmas Eve, their job is to carry the Ocean Elves who hold the waterproof toy bags through the *Christmas Caves*. You see, the *Christmas Caves* are underwater caves that connect to different beaches all over the world. The caves are really a shortcut for the seals and the Ocean Elves. You probably thought Santa carried all the toy bags in his sleigh with his reindeer, didn't you?"

"Well, *yeah*," I said.

"Everyone thinks that, but think about it. That would be a lot of toys in one sleigh if Santa did it that way. The truth is, Zandra leads the other seals who lead the Ocean Elves through the caves. Then the Ocean Elves hide the waterproof toy bags on beaches and other secret locations all over the world. Inside the bags are special bells and when Santa's sleigh is close by the bells ring, revealing the hiding place. Santa then lands his sleigh and reloads and off he goes to his next stop. It's quite an operation."

"Wow! That's pretty amazing. How long has Santa been doing it that way?"

"Ever since Zandra's great-great-great-grandmother, the Seal Queen Zandra, discovered the caves. Now Zandra carries on the family tradition and she is the leader of the seals. She is the *only* seal who knows where every cave leads to, and her job is to make sure the right bags end up on the right beaches."

"Wow, that's an important job," I said.

"Very important. The Christmas routine would be all out of whack without Zandra."

"So, if she has such a big job, what is Bob's job then?"

"Bob is new to Santa's Seals. I think Zandra must've been showing Bob the caves and how to swim through them when Dr. Gloomsday caught them."

"Oh," I said and continued, "so what's in the *Christmas Caves* that is so valuable to Dr. Gloomsday?"

"Well, during the year the *Christmas Caves* are in complete darkness. That way, no scuba divers will ever find them by mistake. But on Christmas Eve, the caves become a whole different place. Multicolored jellyfish from all depths of the ocean swim to the caves to help light them up for that special night. But I hardly think Dr. Gloomsday is after the jellies."

"Well, then what is he after?"

"It has to be the oysters."

"Oysters?"

"Yes, millions and millions of oysters also go to the caves to help light them up to make it easier for the Ocean Elves."

"Oysters. I don't understand."

"These aren't just any oysters. Each oyster that lives in the *Christmas Caves* has a pearl in its shell. When the oysters open their shells, a white glow as beautiful and peaceful as a snowy night shines throughout the caves. But pearls are also worth a lot of money. Maybe Dr. Gloomsday somehow found out about the oysters and that is why he has captured Zandra and Bob. He wants those pearls."

"Or maybe he just wants to ruin Christmas," I said.

Jay snapped his fingers. "Like in all those make-believe Christmas stories people talk about."

"Yup." I nodded.

He stopped the *Merry Movers* truck in front of the aquarium and turned to me. "But there is nothing make-believe about this, Ryder. We can't let Dr. Gloomsday succeed."

I removed the key from my neck and said, "Keep the truck running and in five minutes we won't have to worry about Dr. Gloomsday ever again."

74

It seemed like an easy plan. I would unlock the cage and Zandra and Bob would follow me back to the *Merry Movers* truck where Jay would then drive us all to safety. We figured it was so cold and late at night that Dr. Gloomsday was probably fast asleep dreaming about all the pearls he was going to steal from the cave.

I flipped on my flashlight and walked briskly to the cage.

"Who is that?" I heard Zandra's voice ask.

"It's me, Ryder," I answered as I approached.

"Ryder! Ryder! You came back! You really came back," Zandra exclaimed and then put her fin on Bob and shook him. "Wake up, Bob! Wake up! Ryder is here! He came back for us!"

Bob opened his eyes and jumped a bit when the light from my flashlight blinded him. "What? What? What's going on?"

"It's OK, it's me, Ryder. And it's true. I've come to save you."

Bob was now wide awake. "But how? The gate's locked."

"He's right, Ryder. There's no way you can open the lock."

"Actually, there is one way." I smiled and then showed them the key.

"Oh, my gosh! How did you get a Santa key?" Zandra asked.

"It's a long story, I'll tell you later," I answered as I put the key in and the lock clicked, instantly opening the gate. A second later, the key turned into dust and the green and red particles blew away into the night.

"We have to hurry," I said. "Jay the Elf is waiting for us!"

Zandra and Bob both clapped their fins. "Jay the Elf is here?!"

"You know him?"

"Of course we do. He's the elf-in-training who always says cheese and crackers," Bob said.

I laughed and pointed. "Yup, that's him. He's in that truck over there. He's going to drive you to safety."

Zandra and Bob waddled out of the cage and followed me.

"Your plan is better than I could've dreamed," Zandra said to me when we were inches from the truck.

I was about to smile with satisfaction when I suddenly noticed something strange about the *Merry Movers* truck. The back of the truck looked lower than the front. I flashed my light in that direction and that's when I saw the silver spike in the tire!

"Jay, you have a flat tire!" I yelled up to him.

He rolled down the window. "What?"

"I *said* you have a flat tire!"

"How could that. . . ?" Jay began and stopped. "Oh, no! Look behind you!"

Zandra, Bob, and I all turned our heads around and there, lit up from the yellow headlights, was the evil monster himself—Dr. Gloomsday!

"Did you really think I wouldn't be waiting for you? Ha! Ha! Ha!" He had a laugh that would frighten even a werewolf!

"Run!" I yelled to the seals. They turned and moved along as fast as their fins could take them, which I have to say wasn't fast at all.

"Look at them." Dr. Gloomsday pointed. "Do you really think they can escape me?" He laughed again, lunging forward to grab me. I didn't know what I was going to do. Just as I moved away, Jay the Elf opened the truck's door, hitting Gloomsday and knocking him to the ground. Jay then jumped out of the truck and sat on top of Dr. Gloomsday.

"Run, Ryder! Run!" Jay yelled.

"But what about you?" I shouted.

"Don't worry about me! I'll be OK. Save the seals! Go! Now!"

I nodded and sprinted until I caught up to the seals. I had no idea what I was going to do next because I didn't have a plan. I quickly realized I didn't need one when O'Nel's ice cream truck came screaming around the corner and screeched to a stop in front of us.

The back doors flew open and my uncle Ted hollered to us, "Hurry up! We gotta go! Hurry!"

There was no time to be in shock so I turned to the seals. "It's OK. That's my uncle! He's here to help!"

Zandra and Bob nodded in agreement, hopped on board, and I followed.

"O'Nel, hit it!" my uncle ordered and O'Nel put his foot to the gas pedal and we zoomed off.

When we were in the clear Uncle Ted turned to me. "Ryder, why didn't you come to me about the seals?"

"You know about the seals?" I couldn't believe it.

"Not really. I just know. . . ." He paused. "The seals *can* talk, can't they?"

"How did you know we can talk?" Bob asked.

Uncle Ted's eyes almost popped out of his head and he fell backwards. "It's true. They *can* talk. I knew they could talk because I heard them talking to you today, Ryder. But I really thought it was my imagination."

"It's not your imagination, Ted. We *can* talk," Zandra added.

Uncle Ted then yelled over his shoulder, "Are you hearing this, O'Nel?"

"Yes, Ted." O'Nel looked at him wide-eyed through the rearview mirror. "So I'm not losing my mind after all, but then again, maybe we all are!"

"None of you are losing your mind," Zandra jumped in. "You can hear us because we are Santa's Seals."

"But I thought only kids can hear you, Zandra?" I asked.

"Yes, only good children or good people who haven't lost their childish spirit. It's obvious that your uncle and O'Nel still have their childhood spirit. I understand why O'Nel hasn't lost his spirit. He sells ice cream. He has to act like a child, but what do *you* do for work, Ted?" Zandra asked my uncle.

"I write books for children."

Zandra smiled. "Oh, yes, Ted the children's writer. I know all about you. Santa is a big fan of your work."

"Really? He is?" Uncle Ted couldn't help but grin.

"Yes, he has given many children your books. Now I know why *you* can understand us," Zandra replied. "You haven't forgotten what it's like to be a child. That's an important gift that, unfortunately, not many people have."

I turned to my uncle. "See Uncle Ted, you still have the gift to think like a child."

"Why wouldn't he have that gift? His books are special." Zandra flapped her fins.

I whispered, "Because Uncle Ted has writer's block."

"Oh, I see. Interesting." Zandra nodded. "Well, I don't think he'll have writer's block anymore after this trip."

"And where exactly is this trip?" O'Nel asked as he took a corner and headed along past the lighthouse road.

"Have you ever heard of Muller's Cove?" Zandra asked.

"Yes, I know where that is." O'Nel laughed. "I can't believe I am answering a question from a talking seal."

Zandra laughed, too. "I know, O'Nel, it takes some getting used to. Anyway, if you can get us to Muller's Cove there is a boat that can bring us to a Christmas Cave that Dr. Gloomsday doesn't know about. We don't have time to swim to it, but if you take us to the cove you'll save Christmas!"

"Did you say Christmas Cave?" Uncle Ted and O'Nel asked.

I patted my uncle on the shoulder. "Believe me, it's a long story."

"Well, Muller's Cove is a half-hour away, we've got time," Uncle Ted replied.

"Sure, I'll tell you everything, but where's Bob?" Zandra asked. We all looked around and suddenly saw Bob sticking his head inside the ice cream freezer.

"Bob! Stop that!" Zandra scolded.

Bob popped his head up and there was strawberry ice cream all over his face and whiskers.

"Wow! That was tasty! I'm sorry, Zandra, but we haven't had any food in days and that ice cream tastes amazing." He patted his fin on his belly and asked, "Hey O'Nel, you wouldn't happen to have any ice cream in salmon flavor? Man, do I love salmon!"

All of us couldn't help but laugh and we continued to laugh as we headed for Muller's Cove. Little did we know that Dr. Gloomsday was going to try to end our laughter forever. . . .

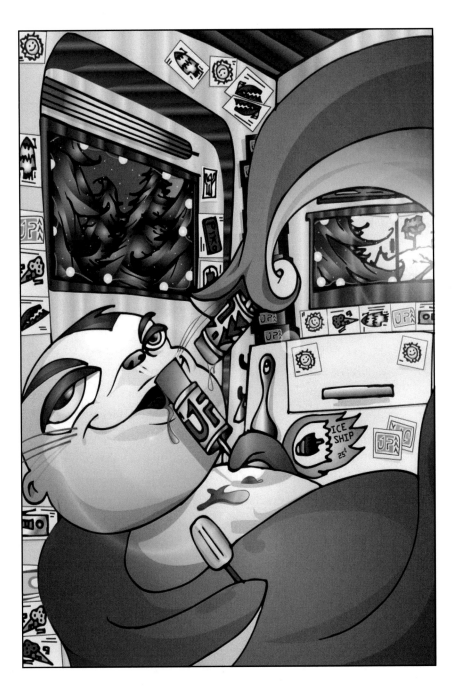

Chapter 8

We entered Muller's Cove just as Zandra finished telling us all about the history of Santa's Seals and the Christmas Caves.

"It's not that I don't believe you, Zandra. I mean you're a talking seal for crying out loud, but why have I never heard of Santa's Seals before?" Uncle Ted asked.

"Yeah, all I've ever heard about were Santa's *reindeer*," O'Nel stressed as he drove along the seashell driveway that led to Romeo's Wharf, the section of the cove where the fishing boats docked.

"Cheese and crackers," Bob exclaimed. "I told you, Zandra, the reindeer always get the credit!"

"And that's quite alright, Bob," she said to him and turned to us. "We don't do our job for credit. We do it for the joy it brings to children. I remember the wonderful feeling I had my first Christmas as I led the Ocean Elves through the tricky caves. A few weeks later, Santa read me some of the thank-you letters he had received from the kids. It was then I knew I was making the world a better place to live in." Zandra smiled but my mind was focused on something I had just heard from Bob.

I snapped my fingers and repeated it. "Cheese and crackers! Speaking of cheese and crackers, what are we going to do about Jay the Elf? Dr. Gloomsday might have caught him or something."

"Don't worry about Jay the Elf. I'm sure he escaped. That's one thing about elves—they can be very slippery when they have to be."

"Seals can be slippery, too," Uncle Ted added. "But you two got caught."

"Yeah, how *did* Dr. Gloomsday capture you?" I asked.

Bob's head lowered and Zandra said, "Well, I guess I just wasn't paying attention."

"You don't have to cover for me, Zandra." Bob patted her fin and said to us, "It was *my* fault."

"Your fault? What did you do?" I asked.

"Zandra was showing me the caves, and we had just come out of one when I saw a submarine above us. I swam closer and noticed the submarine was dropping fish out of a hatch. The fish looked so tasty that I swam even closer. Zandra warned me that it was a trap but I didn't listen to her. I just kept swimming. Before I knew it, I was chewing on a *rubber* fish and a net covered me. Then Zandra tried to bite through the net to free me and that's when another net scooped her up. You see, this whole thing is my fault."

"It's OK, Bob, everything happens for a reason. Something good always comes from something bad." Zandra said.

"Something good?" Bob shook his head. "The only reason this happened was because I'm stupid. I'm *good* at being that! Stupid!"

Zandra slapped her fin on the floor. "Don't ever call yourself stupid, Bob. You're not stupid. You're funny and kind and you made me feel safe when we were caught. I know you're going to make a wonderful Santa Seal. You just made a mistake. Everyone makes mistakes. And you want to know *the* something good that came from this? If you hadn't tried to eat that rubber fish, we wouldn't have met our new friends Ryder, Ted, and O'Nel."

Bob smiled and said, "That's true. I do like them. . . ." and then he clapped his fins. "Hey, everyone, there was also another good thing that came from what happened."

"What's that, Bob?" we all asked.

"If I hadn't got us caught, I wouldn't have been able to eat a tub of strawberry ice cream." He rubbed his belly. "Let me tell you, that ice cream was *no* rubber fish!"

We all laughed, and then O'Nel pointed at the boat in front of us. It didn't look like a boat at all, and it definitely didn't look like a fishing boat. It looked more like an old whaling ship from another time period.

"Is that the ship, Zandra?" O'Nel asked.

Zandra poked her head out the window and squinted. "Yup, there she is. The *Aislynn*. You get us on that ship and Bob and I will be safe."

"The," I sounded the word out, "*Ais-lynn*. I've never heard that name before. What does the name Aislynn mean, Zandra?"

"It's means 'beautiful dream' or 'beautiful vision.' The captain named it after a dream he once had. It was a dream that actually came true," she answered, and I was going to ask her more questions, but O'Nel parked the truck and opened the door.

"All right, let's get Zandra and Bob on board," O'Nel said.

"Yeah, Christmas Eve is only a day away and they have to get back," Uncle Ted agreed.

We all got out of the truck and walked up the gangway onto the *Aislynn*.

"Captain? Captain, are you here?" Zandra called out.

A gruff voice shouted from the pilothouse, "Who dares to board my ship without my permission?"

"Captain, it's me, Zandra."

"Zandra? The Seal Princess Zandra?" His gruffness softened.

"Yes, Captain," she answered.

"Princess, what in blazes are you doing here a day before Christmas Eve?"

"Something has happened and I need your help."

"Alright, I'll be down in a moment."

That moment seemed to take forever, and I finally found out the reason it did when the captain appeared supported by a wooden walking stick. He limped slowly toward us. I first stared at the stick that had carvings of symbols in it. I was trying to make out what those symbols were but then I looked up at the captain and gasped. Actually, we all gasped but it wasn't because the captain was limping. It was because he was an old man who had a long, green, seaweed-colored beard with barnacles and icicles hanging from it.

"Princess, you didn't tell me there were others. Who's the new Santa Seal and who is this motley crew with you?" He waved his walking stick at us.

"The seal is named Bob. And this is O'Nel, Ted, and Ryder. They saved me from the evil Dr. Gloomsday." She pointed her fin at each of us.

He stared at me and his left eye seemed to change colors from blue to red to green like it was a kaleidoscope being adjusted.

Finally he spoke. "Oh, Gloomsday. I've had a few run-ins with that one before. Well, I guess this motley crew is alright if they saved Princess Zandra."

"They are wonderful people and I'll miss them." She turned to me and kissed my cheek.

"Well, I suppose we'll have to get you to a *Christmas*

Cave that Gloomsday doesn't know about. So, please, Seal Princess Zandra, and you too, Bob, finish saying your goodbyes," the captain ordered.

But we were interrupted by the sound of a car horn blaring.

"What is that?" O'Nel asked.

"Look over there!" Uncle Ted pointed at what was barreling into the parking lot on three good wheels—Jay the Elf in the *Merry Movers* truck. He screeched to a stop, jumped out, and ran up the gangway.

"Cheese and . . . cheese and . . . cheese and. . . ." He tried to continue while he caught his breath.

"Crackers!" we all chanted for him.

"Yes! You gotta get out of here! Gloomsday just jumped into his submarine and he's planning on chasing you down!"

"Drop the gangway, Elf!" The captain shouted the order. Jay ran over and pushed the gangway off the ship and onto the dock.

"Wait! We can't go with you!" Uncle Ted protested.

"You have no choice. You're on a mission for Santa now! So pull up that anchor, mate!"

Uncle Ted looked at O'Nel and me for a minute before hollering, "You heard the captain! Let's pull up that anchor!"

All three of us ran over and grabbed the rope, pulling it like we were in a tug-o-war until finally the anchor was out of the water and secured. Then we helped raise the sails and in a matter of seconds we were sailing at a good speed out of the cove and headed for open sea.

"We should be in good shape for a while. There's food below if you're hungry," the captain said.

"Well, I could go for some sardine sandwiches," Bob said as he waddled down the stairs.

"I'm right behind you." Zandra followed.

"Cheese and crackers with sardines? Hmm . . . sounds tasty!" Jay the Elf exclaimed and hustled after them.

O'Nel, Uncle Ted, and I decided to stay on deck.

After we'd sailed for a while, the captain pointed to me. "You. Young man. Your name is Ryder, is it not?"

"Yes, Sir."

"Well, Master Ryder, would you like to take the wheel for a while?"

I looked at Uncle Ted for his approval and he nodded so I replied with joy, "Yes, Sir!"

I ran to the wheel and the captain handed over the duty to me by saying, "Just keep her steady and you'll be doing fine, Master Ryder."

"So, Captain," Uncle Ted said as he walked over, "you said we'll be in good shape. How do you know that, Sir?"

"Yes, how do you know that, Captain?" O'Nel asked.

The captain laughed. "To tell you the truth, I don't know if we will be in good shape but surely that's a better answer than saying we'll be sunk by a cannonball or a sea monster will devour us or Dr. Gloomsday will fire his freeze-ray gun at us. Don't you think?"

"Cannonballs, sea monsters, freeze-ray guns," Uncle Ted repeated and then joined the captain's laughter and then said, "I suppose you're right about that, Sir."

"Please, stop calling me 'Sir'. Call me by name. I am Captain Salty Sam. But you can call me Salty."

"Salty Sam!" Uncle Ted and I shouted together.

"You've heard of me?" he asked in surprise.

"Salty Sam! As mean and salty as a storm at sea!" Uncle Ted and I both replied quickly.

"Well, I guess you *have* heard of me. But I've changed from that old description."

"I know," I interrupted, remembering Uncle Ted's story. "You became a lovable sweet tooth after you discovered the island made out of chocolate."

Salty took his walking stick and poked it under my chin, propping my head up. "How in blazes did you know about the island made out of chocolate?"

In fright, I pointed next to me. "My uncle Ted told me."

Salty moved his stick away from me and onto my uncle. "You told him that?"

"Yes, I did! I'm a writer and it's from a story I made up!"

"A story?" His kaleidoscope eye turned red.

"But it's not true. I made it up. So *this* can't be true! This makes no sense. I *made* it up! You can't be Salty Sam!"

Captain Salty Sam's eye turned green and he laughed. "So, now I understand. You're a *storyteller*."

"Yes, Ted is a storyteller. Why is that so funny?" O'Nel moved forward.

"Yeah, what's so funny about that?" Uncle Ted added.

The captain turned to my uncle. "You see, chances are, Storyteller Ted, your great-granddaddy told your granddaddy about Salty Sam who then told your daddy the story of me, and it's been inside you waiting to get out and now you have passed it on to your nephew where the story now lives and breathes but. . . ." He stopped.

"But what?" we all asked.

"But with every version of a tale there are a few minor changes." Salty then turned to me. "And in this version, Master Ryder, I must add a piece that no one has heard before. It wasn't the chocolate that made me a lovable sweet tooth. Well, I take that back, the chocolate *did* help but it really was Aislynn who shined on my dark spirit and brightened my soul forever."

"Your ship, *Aislynn*?"

"No, I renamed my ship *Aislynn* after I met her. You see my walking stick here?"

"Yes, the one you just poked my uncle and me with," I said.

"Yes, sorry about that. For a moment there, I thought you might be a spy for Gloomsday or worse, a Holiday Pirate."

"A what?" I asked.

"A Holiday Pirate," Captain Salty Sam said.

"What's a Holiday Pirate?"

"I've heard of them from my mother, little Ryder man." O'Nel shook his head from side to side. "They are the worst pirates ever because no matter what the holiday is they try to steal it."

"You are right, O'Nel, they are wicked people, but let's get back to the story of my walking stick."

"Oh, yes," we all replied.

"When I was a little boy my mother and I would wait for days for my father to come home from one of his voyages. To occupy my time, she would tell me stories under our big oak tree that overlooked the ocean. One of the stories was about a beautiful mermaid named Aislynn who guarded an island made out of chocolate. I used to fall asleep under that tree dreaming of the island of chocolate and of Aislynn. It was just a dream. Well, at least I thought it was."

"What do you mean?" I asked.

"Well, when I hurt my leg and eye in a battle with the Holiday Pirates, one I care not to discuss, a man with a long, white beard came to my rescue. He handed me this here oak wood walking stick and said, 'All your answers to happiness are carved in this stick.'" Salty passed the stick to each of us so we could inspect it. There were carvings of a mermaid, an island, and a list of numbers.

"What are those numbers for?" Uncle Ted asked.

"They are coordinates. Marked on this stick is the map to the island made out of chocolate."

"Wow," we all gasped.

"Yes, and when I found the island I quickly realized the man was right."

"How so?" O'Nel asked.

"I *had* never been happier in my life. I ate chocolate for breakfast, lunch, dinner, and of course dessert. I decided I'd live there, and I was going to have all the chocolate I ever wanted, but then I saw her—the mermaid."

"Aislynn?" I asked.

"Indeed. She was swimming with a school of red Swedish fish. She was the most beautiful vision I had ever seen. Aislynn told me my true happiness would never come from consuming all the chocolate. I would just end up with a sick tummy. No, my happiness would only be discovered when I shared it with the rest of the world. At first, I thought that meant I was supposed to share my discovery, but then she told me there was only one person I could trust who would keep the chocolate special. And it was the same person who had trusted me."

"Who? The man with the long, white beard?" I asked.

"Yes, the man with the long white beard, but you probably know him better as Santa Claus."

"Santa Claus!" Our mouths fell open.

"Yes, Santa Claus gave me the map because it was his hope that through this bad eye I would see the true beautiful meaning of Christmas, and I have. I use my ship the *Aislynn* once every year to carry the chocolate from the island to the North Pole so it can be used as Christmas candy that my friend good Old Jolly leaves in the children's stockings."

"Unbelievable," I said.

Salty laughed and repeated, "*Unbelievable.* Now that's a word I no longer *believe* in! Am I correct, Storyteller Ted?"

My uncle didn't reply because he couldn't! Out of nowhere, a blast of ice and snow flew over the bow and froze him instantly!

"Uncle Ted!" I felt his stone-colored face and realized he had just been turned into an ice statue!

"Oh, no! It's Gloomsday! He's shooting his freeze-ray gun from his submarine! Hurry! Pull on those sails! Zandra! Bob! Elf! Get up here!"

"You mean he *really* has a freeze-ray gun?!" O'Nel shouted, but just as the words left his lips, he too was hit and turned into an ice statue.

"Oh, no! Are they going to be OK? Oh, no! What are we going to do, Captain?" I hollered.

"They'll be fine. All we have to do is sail. . . ." Salty didn't finish his sentence because another blast of ice shot over the bow and froze him beside the wheel.

"Oh, no!" I screamed, staring at the three ice statues.

Zandra, Bob, and Jay the Elf finally appeared.

"It's Gloomsday!" I shouted to them.

"What are we going to do?" Bob asked while dodging the flying ice.

"Cheese and crackers with ice cubes!" Jay hollered.

"It's going to be OK." Zandra said calmly.

"It is?" We all turned to her.

"Yes. Ryder will figure something out."

"I will?" I asked, almost freezing, not from the freeze-ray gun but from fear!

"Yes. Believe in yourself, Ryder, as much as I believe in you, and we will all be safe."

It was the last thing Zandra said before turning into the fourth frozen statue!

Chapter 9

"Don't worry, Ryder, if we can let Santa know what's happened to your uncle and Zandra and the others, he'll be able to unfreeze them, and it will be like nothing ever happened." Bob tried calming me down while I took cover, huddling under the wheel.

"Bob, how can I not worry? Look at my uncle Ted! He's a human popsicle!"

Jay interrupted, pointing at the submarine that was now above water and speeding in our direction. "Glooms-day's gaining on us!"

"Duck!" I yelled as another blast of ice from the sub's gun flew over our heads and froze the main deck, turning it into a skating rink.

I realized I had no time to think about Uncle Ted or the others, and I definitely didn't have time to be afraid. I jumped up, grabbed the wheel, and turned it hard to the right. Everyone, even the four frozen statues, tilted with the ship to the side, and this time when the gun fired, the ice missed us, instead freezing the ocean beside the ship.

"Good move, Ryder!" Bob hollered.

"Thanks!" I let myself take a quick breath and it *was* quick because the gun fired again, this time freezing the ocean on the other side of the ship, making it so we could not turn right or left. I looked over my shoulder and saw the gun's barrel adjusting and pointing toward the sky. It looked like Gloomsday was aiming to fire the ice beyond the ship.

"Why would he do tha. . . ?" I began but Jay put it together.

"Oh, no! Ryder! Bob! Gloomsday's going to try to trap us by freezing the ocean around the ship!" Jay pointed at the ice closing in on us.

"We'll just have to outrun him then!" I tried to sound brave and stay focused on the ocean in front of me, and that's when I noticed it.

"What's that white light up ahead?" I asked.

With his left hand above his eyes, Jay squinted. "What white light?"

"That one." I pointed. "It looks like a buoy or something."

When we got closer, I continued, "Yeah, it's a buoy with a lit-up Christmas wreath attached to it."

"You found one!" Bob exclaimed.

"Found one what?"

"A *Christmas Cave*! That buoy marks the entrance to one of the caves!"

"But it can't be. I don't see any land around here!" I said.

"Just because we can't see land doesn't mean there isn't any. We're going to be safe now. I'll just swim through the cave and get help from Santa! He'll be here in no time!"

"But Bob, that's exactly what Gloomsday. . . ." Jay and I began. But before we could finish our sentence, Bob slid along the icy deck and belly flopped overboard into the water beyond the ship.

"That's exactly what Gloomsday wants us to do. Lead him to a cave." Jay and I said it again, this time finishing the sentence.

"What are we going to do now, Ryder?"

"I really don't know," I answered, realizing the sub was no longer chasing us. In fact, it had vanished.

"Where'd Gloomsday go?" I asked.

"Look." Jay pointed beyond the ship where the sub suddenly resurfaced. A second later, the gun's barrel swiveled around, aimed and fired. The ice crashed against the front of the ship, knocking Jay and me off balance. Then it fired again at the ocean in the ship's path, freezing the water solid. Now there was ice all around the ship.

"Oh, no!" Jay and I shouted, realizing we were now completely trapped.

We slipped and slid along the deck until we reached the edge. Looking down, we watched the sub's hatch open, and saw Dr. Gloomsday pop his head up before climbing out. He was wearing scuba diving gear and he was carrying an empty red-and-gold colored bag.

"How did Gloomsday get that?" Jay asked.

"What? That bag?"

"Yes, *that* bag! It's red and gold and that means only one thing. It's one of Santa's magical waterproof Christmas bags, but a red and gold one is even more special than the rest of Santa's bags. It's designed to expand and hold anything in the world."

"What do you mean anything?"

"I mean *anything*! If Santa wanted to give an airline jet to a little boy or girl for Christmas, that bag could hold it and it wouldn't even hurt Santa's back when he carried it."

"How's that possible?" I asked.

"He's Santa Claus. He doesn't tell all of his secrets about how he makes Christmas so special for the world. It would take the fun away if we all knew how he does everything. But I do know Santa only uses those kinds of bags when he gives big gifts to towns and villages. Like last year, Santa carried a swimming pool in a red and gold bag to a village in a desert in Egypt. He didn't even break a sweat!"

"Wow!"

"Yes, wow! You know what this means, Ryder?"

"No. What?"

"Gloomsday will be able to carry every single pearl in that bag from every single cave! Not only will he be rich and *this* Christmas be ruined, but the lights could be out for *EVERY* Christmas! We have to do something!"

"Wait!" I snapped my fingers. "Since Salty's ship carries the Christmas chocolate, there must be a radio or something below deck we can use to contact Santa."

I didn't wait for Jay's reply. I turned from him and took a running head-first slide across the icy deck, got up, and went down the ladder two steps at a time.

When I got below deck, my eyes searched while my hands threw ropes, fishing gear, and life jackets aside.

"There has to be some way to stop Gloomsday," I said and pushed a table of boxes aside to give me space to enter the next room. But when a few of the boxes fell off the table I noticed a red, metal door with a big round handle. Next to the handle was a keypad for the combination. The lock was designed for letters and not for numbers.

The door really looked like it should be for a safe in a bank or something and not on an old ship. I wondered briefly if Captain Salty Sam kept treasure in the vault; but then I noticed large initials engraved in gold lettering.

"O.E.," I said out loud.

"O.E.," Jay repeated as he hopped down the ladder

and ran over to me. "It means Ocean Elves! Good work, Ryder! I bet there's a direct line to Santa behind that door or maybe a jet ski or something."

"Jet ski?"

"Yeah, the Ocean Elves use jet skis sometimes when they're working or just to have fun in the summertime. Turn the handle and find out."

"It's not that easy." I pointed at the key pad. "It's a lock that has a four-letter combination."

"Of course it does. I should've known," Jay said.

"How should you have known?"

"It's clear that Santa installed this because all of his locks have letter combinations. All the combinations spell out words that deal with Christmas. So, we have to think of a four-letter word. Wait, I got it! Try the word 'Tree.'"

I nodded and pegged the letters T-R-E-E, then spun the handle and pulled.

"Still locked," I said, and tried to think. "Wait, I got it." I pushed the letters on the keypad that spelled the word 'SNOW' and spun the handle again and pulled.

"Nothing!" I said, frustrated.

"Where are you guys?!!" I heard Bob's voice holler from above the ladder entrance.

"Bob?" Jay looked at me.

"What's he doing here? He should've been halfway to the North Pole by now!" I exclaimed.

"Ryder! Jay! Where are you? I need your help!" Bob yelled again.

I turned from the safe and followed Jay up the ladder.

"Bob, what are you doing here?" I asked.

He pointed his fin behind him.

"Ryder, that was an old *Christmas Cave* no longer in use. I was swimming and I came to a wall of burning, red coal and couldn't get by it. It was a dead end."

"That's OK," I said, "I think we found a safe and if we open it we—"

"We have to help Gloomsday!" Bob interrupted.

"Huh?" Jay and I both shrugged.

"When I swam back I saw Gloomsday at the entrance of the cave. He caught his legs in black coal rocks."

"Why would coal be underwater?" I was confused.

"I don't understand either, but there are piles of it on his legs. Anyway, I tried to push him free but he's really stuck. If we don't help him soon he could be down there forever!"

"I saw some rope below." I turned and almost bumped into my frozen friend O'Nel.

I looked at O'Nel's face and suddenly it came to me.

"I've got it! I've got it!" I shouted, and ran.

"Got what?" Jay followed.

I climbed down the ladder but this time I used three steps at a time!

After I sprinted over to the red door, I took a deep

breath and said to Jay, "What's another way to say Christmas?"

He shrugged. "You got me."

I punched the letters **N-O-E-L.**

"Noel," I said and spun the handle, pulled the door, and this time it unlocked!

"Ryder, you did it! You did it!" He patted me on the back.

When I opened the door I expected to see a jet ski or a radio; but I was wrong. There was something on a hanger but it was no clothes monster! It was a red scuba diving suit with white O.E. initials on the front of it.

"Wow! That's an Ocean Elves scuba suit! Those suits can keep you warm in any type of weather."

"Great! Jay, you put the suit on. Then I'll give you the rope and you can swim down with Bob and tie it to Gloomsday. I'll stay on deck and we can pull him loose."

"Ryder, that's a great plan, except for one thing," Jay said.

"What's that?"

"I can't swim."

"What do you mean, you can't swim?" I said.

"I *mean* I can't swim! I'm trying to be a regular elf, not an *ocean* one! What are we going to do now?"

I wish my parents were here, I thought, they would know what to do! But I had to make this decision on my own! I studied the scuba suit and realized it was not only made for an elf but it was also made for an eight-year-old boy!

"Take the rope and tie it to the ship and tell Bob I'll be right up," I ordered.

"And what are you going to do?" Jay asked.

"I'm going to try and save Gloomsday," I said, grabbing the scuba suit.

I had no idea what I was about to face, but I did know that my secret journey wasn't over. It was about to continue under the sea!

Chapter 10

I had gone scuba diving with my parents and Uncle Ted hundreds of times before, but I had never gone alone, and I had *never* gone diving to try and rescue some crazy guy who had tried to freeze me! So, yeah, I guess I was a little nervous standing on the ice staring at the gloomy waves lapping below me.

"Are you sure you want to do this?" Jay hollered from above and threw me the rope after he had tied his end of it to the *Aislynn*.

"So are you saying I have a choice?" I asked.

"Well, no. Not really."

"Great. I didn't think so."

Bob, who was already in the water, urged me on by saying, "Zandra believes in you and so do I. So now it's time for you, Ryder Matthews, to believe in yourself."

"Bob, I appreciate the pep talk but my biggest fear really isn't going under water. I'm more worried that I won't be able to see anything once I get down there."

"What do you mean?"

"Well, since we found out this *Christmas Cave* is no longer in use there are probably no oyster pearls to light up the ocean."

"You're right. But Dr. Gloomsday got his legs trapped outside the cave, so there should be plenty of light for you to use."

"Bob, I don't understand. It's not like I have a flashlight or anything. It might not be *as* dark, but it will *still* be dark."

"Trust me, Ryder. Jump in and you'll see what I mean about you having enough light."

"OK. This is crazy. I'm standing here arguing with a talking seal," I said to myself and threw my hands up in defeat.

I also realized that every second I spent asking Bob a question was another second of oxygen lost from Gloomsday's tank, so I placed my hand over my mask and did a diver's backwards roll into the ocean.

Bob had been right about the scuba suit being warm. I felt like I had just dived into bath water and not the icy, bone-chilling winter ocean. The comfort made me feel safe, but then my heart skipped a beat when I realized Bob *had* been wrong about something. I couldn't see a thing! I couldn't even make out my own hands as I used them to push through the water while I flapped my flippers, heading *hopefully* down to the *Christmas Cave.*

There was no way I'd be able to find Gloomsday. I mean, I had already lost Bob in the black water. But just as I was thinking I was on a hopeless mission, the O and E on my scuba suit switched on and the letters were like nightlights in a dark hallway. I saw the power from the bright white O and E lights in front of me, and it seemed they were more like headlights on a car. They shined on the ocean, lighting it up like it was an empty highway.

But the ocean was far from empty. There were schools of fish of all sizes and colors.

It *is* a highway, I thought, an *ocean* highway.

Little fish darted past me like they were commuters in the speed lane during rush hour, while some bigger ones cruised along at a leisurely pace, reminding me of my grandparents taking me on a Sunday drive. The only difference with *this* highway was that the schools of fish weren't headed in the same direction. Their beautiful multicolors zig-zagged all around me. I almost got lost in the beauty of the moment, but then I spotted something approaching me from the bottom of the ocean. It was a large, round figure. My breathing slowed and my muscles tensed. It looked like the outline of a person.

Oh, no, I thought, maybe Gloomsday has shaken himself loose, and instead of thanking me, he's now coming after me! The figure swam closer.

What was I going to do? I closed my eyes for a moment and tried to calm down. When I opened them, I was nose to nose with the face.

"Aggh," I exclaimed, but then chuckled when I realized that it wasn't the evil Dr. Gloomsday but a bored, maybe even annoyed-looking sea turtle.

"Hey, elf, some of us are trying to sleep down here. Don't you know how to use those lights? You got the high beams on. Man, I only moved here because I thought you elves no longer came around these parts." The sea turtle grumbled as he swam slowly past me.

As Bob came my way, he glanced at the turtle and laughed. "Sounds like your suit has that turtle fooled. You're a regular Ocean Elf now."

I was still a little dazed from just hearing a turtle *speak* to me, so I shook my head from side to side in amazement.

"What's the matter, Ryder? Did you think only seals could talk?"

"Well, yeah," I tried to reply but what came out was nothing but bubbles.

"Whoops. Sorry. I forgot that you can't talk underwater. Follow me. The cave is over there." Bob directed his fin to where I detected the shadow of the cave in the distance. He took the lead and I followed.

When we arrived outside the cave, I could see a frightened Dr. Gloomsday struggling to free his legs from a mound of coal piled over them. Resting next to him on the coal was Santa's magical red and gold bag.

"Dr. Gloomsday, I know you can't understand me but I brought help." Bob pointed over at me and I showed Gloomsday the rope.

Gloomsday squinted but then put it together, nodded enthusiastically, and grabbed for the rope, which I handed to him.

Bob patted me with his fin. "OK, Ryder, remember the plan. I'm going to swim up and tell Jay that Gloomsday has the rope. When Jay starts pulling, I'll swim back down here and try pushing the doctor while you also try to pull him loose."

I nodded OK and briefly watched Bob swim off before turning back to Gloomsday. I noticed something in his eyes that I hadn't seen before. They looked sad and somehow they spoke to me. I felt like he was using them to tell me that he was sorry for what he had done to us, but I couldn't be positive because Gloomsday's eyes then turned as big and round as black bowling balls. He took his hands off the rope and pointed behind me in Bob's direction.

I wanted to tell him, "Don't worry, Bob's not leaving us here," but I would have swallowed a mouth full of seawater.

So, since I couldn't respond with words, I pointed above me, and then like a street mime I pointed at the rope and made a pulling motion. But my body language still didn't make him understand our plan to free him, because he shook his head wildly and again wagged his finger behind me. This time he was frantic.

I looked over my shoulder and spotted the outline of two figures swimming in our direction.

Oh, that's what he was pointing at, I thought, the sea turtle must have a buddy. I laughed to myself, realizing Gloomsday was having the same reaction I had earlier. I turned around to calm him down when my eyes caught the figures speeding past me. They headed right for Gloomsday but then slammed head first into the coal rocks beside him. The cave shook and it felt like an underwater earthquake as a blast of water shot me several yards away from the cave. After a minute, I shook my head, fixed my mask, and realized something.

Those were *not* annoyed sea turtles. But what were they?

I got my answer when the figures swam around in a circle, ready to make another run at Gloomsday.

The answer screamed in my head, OH, NO! HAMMERHEAD SHARKS!

I didn't know what to do and more thoughts pounded my head like angry surf. Should I try to distract them so they don't attack Gloomsday? But then what would I do when they chased me? Is there any way I can out-swim them and live to tell the tale?

Then a random thought struck me: What are hammerhead sharks doing here in such cold water? Didn't Mrs. McDonald just teach us that hammerhead sharks like warm water?

"Very good. Mrs. McDonald must be a wonderful teacher," I heard a sweet voice from behind me say.

I turned around and there in front of me was one of the most beautiful visions I had ever seen. Her hair swirled in red and white like the colors of a candy cane, and she smiled at me with emerald green eyes that matched her long tail, which she moved slowly from side to side.

Aislynn, the mermaid, my mind spoke the name in awe.

"Yes, Aislynn is my name. And when I just said "very good" to you, I meant very good that you knew my friends the hammerheads normally don't enjoy cold water. That means you listen in school. My friends Hank and Harold are only here to help shake that pile of coal off Dr. Gloomsday and set him free."

I couldn't believe what the mermaid was saying to me because I *hadn't* said anything to her. I had only *thought* those things!

"Don't be alarmed, little Ryder. I know you can't talk underwater but that doesn't mean you can't communicate with me. You see, when a person is underwater, I can understand whatever he thinks about. I guess you could say I read minds. So, if you have any questions just think about them and I'll be happy to answer you."

OK, how did you know about Dr. Gloomsday, I thought as I watched the hammerheads slam into the pile again, knocking more coal off his legs.

"I've met Dr. Gloomsday before. Actually, I've met him twice. I first met Phocas when he was a little boy and just like you, he was scuba diving."

Phocas?

"Phocas is Dr. Gloomsday's first name. Oh, how little Phocas loved the ocean. It was for that reason I approached him underwater and told him that when he grew up he should consider becoming a doctor of the ocean to make the ocean a better place for everyone."

Well, he did become a doctor, Aislynn, but it doesn't look like he wants to make the ocean a better place. What happened to him?

"Yes, it's really quite sad. I read his mind as I am reading yours right now, and back then, it really seemed that he did want to make the world a better place, but what happened to him happens to many children when they grow up."

What is that?

"They forget."

Forget what?

"They forget the joy that comes from their childhood dreams. I wish the doctor would remember who he was, little Phocas, the boy who loved the sea and not the Gloomsday he has become. I wonder little Ryder, will that happen to you? Will you forget the joy that comes from your dreams? Will you forget what a great gift it is to be a child?"

I hope not.

"That is promising because it's an honest answer. That means honesty flows throughout your soul. There is hope if you can keep your child's spirit in your heart. Most children I ask that question of answer it by saying, 'I will never forget.' But they do forget." Aislynn pointed over at Dr. Gloomsday, who was now free and rubbing his legs.

"But the truth is," she continued, "we can never really know the answer to that question until the day we grow old. That will be the day we know if we really have stayed young. Ryder, the trick is to always fight to keep that child in your heart and to never forget the joy that comes from your childhood dreams."

I will try, Aislynn.

"Good boy." Aislynn then motioned with her tail and out of the shadows swam three red fish carrying the red and gold Santa bag. The fish that resembled Swedish candy fish opened their mouths and the bag floated into my hands.

Aislynn motioned over at Gloomsday, who was fixing his mask.

She continued, "I met Dr. Gloomsday for the second time the other day. The problem was he was no longer a little boy and this time I was not under water. I was lying on a rock when his submarine found me."

Why was that a problem?

"This time when I talked with him I couldn't read his mind. You see, without his thoughts I had to trust his words. I told him how I had just found this bag in one of the Christmas Caves. I also told him that it was very important to Santa and asked if he could return it to Zandra since he was heading in her direction."

You know Zandra?

"Yes. It is my job to know all of the ocean's creatures and where they are at all times. So I sent Dr. Gloomsday directly to where Zandra and Bob were swimming. He didn't fail Santa—he failed himself. Now I give the bag to you. It is your mission, Ryder, to get this bag and the seals back to Santa in time for Christmas. Can you do it?"

I wasn't sure if I answered Aislynn in my mind or not. I never knew because in an instant the three Swedish fish, the two hammerhead sharks, and the beautiful mermaid Aislynn had all disappeared. All that remained was Dr. Gloomsday, who now had recovered and was swimming with a head of steam straight for me. What am I going to do now? my mind asked, hoping Aislynn would reply but knowing it was now up to me to find the answer!

Chapter 11

There was only one answer I could come up with when Gloomsday rocketed through the water and headed straight for me.

That answer was a simple one.

Run!!! Or in my case, *swim*!!!

Holding Santa's bag in one hand, I turned away, kicked my fins, and raced for the surface. I knew if I could find Bob or get to the ship where Jay was waiting I'd be safe. Without his freeze-ray gun, there was no way Gloomsday would be able to overpower the three of us. At least, that's what I was hoping as I swam to the top. I still had one problem—fear. Instead of fear driving me on, it was actually zapping my energy. It got worse when I felt Gloomsday gaining, but then a vision came to me. It was a memory of the previous summer.

I was competing in a swim meet, racing against the fastest swimmer from my town. The memory played back in my mind as I pointed my one free hand above my head, cupped the water, and kicked away. I could see and hear my parents cheering me on. The fear suddenly vanished as I kicked even harder, pretending that I was back there in that pool on the day I won the blue ribbon.

I broke through the surface of the water and expected applause, but then looked around and was back in the moment.

I ripped my breathing piece out of my mouth and yelled, "Help! Help! Jay! Help!"

Jay didn't respond because he couldn't. There was no way he could hear me since I had come up in front of the submarine and not near the ice in front of the ship. I would have to swim over to that area and pull myself up on the ice, I thought, but I knew I didn't have enough strength to do that. I also didn't want to drop the bag. I needed help.

"Bob! Bob! Where are you?" My eyes desperately searched the ocean, but there was no sign of him.

Suddenly, a hand shot up out of the water and clutched my shoulder, dragging me under for a second. I pushed my head up above the waves, spat up some sea water, and was face to face with Gloomsday!

"Agggh!" I screamed.

His breathing piece was out of his mouth and he yelled back, "No! No! No!"

"Agggh!" I punched wildly away with my free hand, trying to shake him loose.

"No! Please!" He released his hold. "I just needed some support to help me out of the water. I'm not going to hurt you! I promise!"

"You froze my uncle and my friends! And I'm supposed to trust *you*!"

"Yes, Ryder, please trust me. I'm sorry for what I've done." Dr. Gloomsday's face was pale and his voice sounded sad and broken, but how *could* I trust him?

I added, "Not to mention you just chased me!"

"I only chased you because my tank ran out of air. I couldn't hold my breath any longer. I knew if you swam really fast to the top I could follow your lead. You have to believe me. I know that what I have done to you and the others is horrible. I realize what I've become and I don't like it."

While I treaded water using Santa's bag as a flotation device, I wondered what to do. I realized the situation was similar to my run-in with Jay the Elf. Should I trust him like I had trusted Jay? That worked out in the end. Of course, Jay hadn't turned Uncle Ted into *Uncle Ice Bar*!

"Please Ryder, tell me, you spoke to Aislynn, didn't you?" he asked softly.

I put my thoughts aside and answered, "Yes. I did."

"What did she say? Did she hear me thinking down

there? I was trying to speak to her with my thoughts. I was trying to apologize to her. Does she know I now realize what a terrible person I have become?" Dr. Gloomsday asked the questions, but I couldn't answer them because just then Bob popped his head out of the water. He moved quickly like a superhero, wrapping his fins around Gloomsday, yelling, "OK, Dr. Mean Guy, I saw you chasing Ryder down there! We were going to give you a second chance but not now, Buddy!"

I waved my hand. "It's OK, Bob. It's OK."

"What do you mean it's OK? He just. . . ."

"Just let him go and let's all get back on the ship. Dr. Gloomsday and I can explain everything when we get there."

"Yes, please tell the seal to stop barking at me."

"Barking? I'm *talking* here, Buddy, but you can't understand me, can you?" Bob got in his face.

"Please tell him to let me go!" Gloomsday begged me.

I gave Bob a stern look and said, "Let him go, Bob."

"Alright." He reluctantly took his fins off Gloomsday.

The three of us swam over to the ice platform. After we all got out of the water, we went over to the ship and climbed aboard.

"You rescued him! But you didn't use the rope! What happened?" Jay asked as we reached the deck with Gloomsday.

"It's a long. . . ." I began.

"Story," Jay filled in the sentence. "I know. I know it *always* is."

"But it's true. We don't have time to talk," I said to Jay and handed him the bag.

I turned to Dr. Gloomsday. "We need to unfreeze everyone. You do have that kind of machine on your submarine, right?"

Gloomsday walked over and inspected my frozen uncle, then O'Nel, and Salty Sam, and finally stopped in front of Zandra. Then he walked to the side of the ship, looked out at the horizon, and buried his head in his hands and began crying. I noticed one teardrop run down his face and fall into the ocean.

I slid across the deck and said, "You can fix this, right? You have to fix this, Doctor!"

"A mechanism on my freeze-ray gun broke when I was firing at you. I can't reverse the process. I . . I . . . I can't fix this." He hung his head over the side of the balcony and more of his tears fell into the sea.

I looked over at my uncle and my frozen friends. I was beyond words and completely helpless. But then I noticed something about the ocean. At the very point where Dr. Gloomsday's tears landed a small cloud of gray mist had formed. The cloud then turned into the bright colors of a rainbow and expanded into the shape of a woman.

"Who is that?" Bob asked, pointing his fin at the beautiful rainbow-colored woman who hovered above the ship like a ghost that had risen from the ocean.

Dr. Gloomsday raised his head and his eyes widened at the sight. "It can't be her!"

"Who?" Jay, Bob, and I asked.

"Queen Thunderbolt," he whispered, but then shouted to the ghost, "Is it you? Is it really you, Queen Thunderbolt?"

The rainbow-colored ghost nodded and floated closer to the ship.

"Who is Queen Thunderbolt?" I asked.

"My grandfather was a fisherman when I was a little boy and he would go on long voyages to Alaska. When he came home at Christmas time, he'd sit me on his lap and tell me many tales of the sea. My favorite story was how his boat had been trapped in ice for 40 days. He thought that would be his resting place, but then she appeared." Dr. Gloomsday pointed at the ghost. "Queen Thunderbolt! My Grandpa had heard many legends about her saving lost ships but he always thought they were just fish tales. But on that day, there she was, as bright and colorful as a rainbow. She shot thunder and lightning out of her hands and cracked the ice and saved my Grandpa, who then returned home to pass on the story to me. I haven't thought of her since I was a child."

We didn't say a word. We just listened as Gloomsday spoke to the ghost in the sky. "And now, Queen Thunderbolt, you are going to save these people and free the *Aislynn* so we can go and tell others how you saved us!"

Queen Thunderbolt smiled down at us. It was quiet and peaceful but then the sound of thunder rocked the ship from side to side, and the ice around it cracked, turning into ice flows that floated away. The ship was free!

I looked to see if my uncle and the others were also free, but they were still frozen statues. I raised my head to ask Queen Thunderbolt for help, and that's when she sent blasts of lightning out of her hands, shooting them directly at Uncle Ted, O'Nel, Salty Sam, and Zandra, and freeing them all from their icy coffins!

"I've never been so cold in my life. I have icicles growing in my hair." O'Nel shook his head from side to side.

"I can't believe how cold I am." Uncle Ted shivered, and I ran over and hugged him. "Uncle Ted! Uncle Ted! You're OK!"

"Yes, Buddy, I'm fine. But what happened?"

Dr. Gloomsday came forward. "I did a terrible thing. I shot my freeze-ray gun and froze all of you. I'm sorry."

Everyone was quiet. No one knew how to respond.

"Well. . . ." Salty paused and then spoke for the group. "At least, now I have more icicles for my beard. How did my old bones thaw out?"

"Queen Thunderbolt saved you!" I pointed to the sky

but she was no longer there. There was just a puffy rainbow cloud surrounding all of us.

"Queen who?" O'Nel asked.

"Queen Thunderbolt," Salty said, rubbing the icicles attached to his beard. "I know of the queen who helps the sailors. In fact, some think that's where I first got my icicles, from another time when she helped me, but I have never had the pleasure of seeing her in person. Who was able to get her here to save us?"

I pointed at the doctor. "Phocas."

"What did you call him?" everyone asked.

"Phocas."

"Did you say Phocas?" Zandra and Bob exchanged curious glances.

"Yes, that's the doctor's first name."

Dr. Gloomsday came over to me. "How did you know that was my name?"

"Aislynn told me," I said.

"You saw Aislynn too?" Salty Sam asked.

"Yes, it's a. . . ."

"Long story," Jay filled in the sentence for me.

"What else did Aislynn say to you?" Dr. Gloomsday asked.

"She told me she wished you would remember who you were, little Phocas, the little boy who loved the sea, and not the man you've become."

Dr. Gloomsday dropped his head in shame, and I

knew he should no longer feel that way.

"But you see, Doctor," I began, "you may think you have forgotten that child inside you, but you just *did* remember the little Phocas inside your heart because you remembered the story of Queen Thunderbolt. You remembered her. You remembered Queen Thunderbolt!"

He raised his head and a smile broke across his face. "I did remember her. Didn't I?"

"Yes, that was when you were happiest." I looked up at Uncle Ted. "and that's what you should remember too, Uncle Ted. You are happiest when you are having fun just telling or writing stories for children. You can't stop doing that no matter what anybody tells you."

"You are so right, my wise little nephew." Uncle Ted patted my shoulder.

"Thanks," I said.

"Hey, but what is that suit you're wearing?" He pointed.

I thumbed over to Jay and he said, "It's a long story!"

We all laughed. But then Zandra, who had been quiet, moved forward. "May I ask the doctor a question?"

"You really *can* talk!" the doctor exclaimed.

Zandra smiled. "That is another good sign you are on your way back to being a good person, Dr. *Phocas*. Yes, Dr. Phocas, I think that should be your name from now on."

"I would like that." Dr. Phocas smiled.

"And now for my question." Zandra took a thoughtful breath. "May I ask you how you came to have the name Phocas?"

"After my grandfather returned from one of his voyages and just before I was born, he suggested that name. Why do you ask?"

"Do you know what it means?" Bob gestured with his fin.

"No. Once I asked him the meaning when I was little and he said one day I would find out, but as I grew older I never thought of it again. Why, what *does* my name mean?"

"Phocas is the Latin word meaning seal. You see, deep down, Doctor, you are one of Santa's Seals meant to do good in this world. But you just had to see it in yourself. You see, everyone is capable of being a Santa Seal. Everyone is capable of making the world a better place to live in. Your job is to open the aquarium and make it a wonderful place for both the animals and children to enjoy."

Dr. Phocas chuckled with joy. "Well, if I'm one of Santa's Seals, then you can count me in on that and my other job!"

"The other job?" O'Nel asked.

"To help all of you save Christmas." Dr. Phocas laughed even louder and we all joined in, thinking that was exactly what we all had just done—saved Christmas.

Of course, none of us noticed that the rainbow-colored cloud that had surrounded the ship had changed colors, or that it was no longer one cloud. It was several black clouds or maybe I should describe them as several clouds that were black as *coal*! Yes, little did any of us know, Christmas was still far from being saved!

Chapter 12

"Well, since Christmas is now saved, does this mean I can finally go home and sit by my warm fireplace?" O'Nel asked Salty as the rest of us stood on the deck talking and laughing with one another and recapping the wild events.

"Sure, if Dr. Phocas doesn't mind taking you folks home," the captain replied.

"I would be honored to." The doctor motioned to the submarine.

"That will be a big help because the seals, Jay the Elf, and Ryder and I have to get going, and I have to turn this ship on to Santa speed so we can get to the North Pole."

"Whoa, what do you mean, *Ryder* has to get going?" my uncle asked, stepping forward.

"Santa is going to want to thank Ryder personally for saving us," Zandra said, and tussled my hair with her fin.

I couldn't believe it. I thought, I'm going to meet Santa Claus!

"Well, I can't let my nephew go alone."

"Yeah, can't Uncle Ted come with me? Please?" I asked.

"I'm sorry, but other than elves, no adults are allowed in *Santa's Village*. It's a strict rule, and there are no exceptions." Zandra shook her head.

"It's true," Salty added. "They don't even allow me to dock there, and I'm in charge of supplying their chocolate, and as Ryder found out, I've also been known to transport some of the *Ocean Elves*."

"I'm not so sure about this."

"Don't worry, Storyteller Ted, I will drop your nephew off in a safe area and the seals and Jay will take him to the village."

"Yes, I'll make sure we get him to *Santa's Village* safely," Jay promised.

"Me, too." Bob put his right fin up.

"Me three," Zandra voiced and added, "Unless, Ted, you don't want Ryder to meet Santa?"

Uncle Ted looked at my pleading eyes and then at the group and finally said, "I'd be a pretty lousy uncle to tell my nephew he couldn't go to *Santa's Village* and meet Santa Claus! Don't you think?"

"Yeah!" Everyone cheered and slapped my uncle on the back.

"But tell Santa that Ryder's parents are going to be staying at my house, so he has to get Ryder back on Christmas Eve before they get there. I really don't think if I told them I let their son go on a trip with a green bearded captain, an elf who says 'cheese and crackers,' and two talking seals that they'd ever believe me. I almost still don't believe it myself!"

Everyone laughed as I hugged my uncle goodbye.

Dr. Phocas put out his hand. "Thank you, Ryder, thank you for showing me the way back to Christmas."

I just smiled and shook his hand and then the doctor shouted to my uncle and O'Nel, "All aboard!"

"C'mon, O'Nel, we have to get going," Uncle Ted said to O'Nel, who was whispering something to Zandra and Bob.

"I'm coming. I just wanted to pass on my wish."

"What wish is that?" I asked.

"My wish for what I want for Christmas, little Ryder man. It's a good one! See you soon." He smiled before climbing into the submarine.

A moment later, the submarine grumbled to life and then plunged under the sea, headed back to Cape Cod.

When the submarine was gone, Salty got serious. He turned to Bob. "Is it true what I heard you say about that Christmas Cave?"

"Is *what* true?" Bob asked.

"That it was coal on Dr. Phocas' legs and when you came to that dead end there was burning red coal?"

"Yes, why?"

"This isn't good." Salty then turned to Zandra and shook his head. "Somehow Zandra, I must've sailed us off course. It *is* close by."

"What's close by? What's going on?" Jay, Bob, and I all asked.

Salty ignored us. He took out his long spyglass and pointed it in front of him and squinted to take a look.

"Yup, just as I feared, the clouds are gathering."

"Yeah, I noticed storm clouds, too," Jay added.

"Those are more than just storm clouds." Zandra sounded nervous.

"What kind of clouds are they, then?" I asked.

"Those clouds cover an island. See it for yourself, Ryder." Salty handed me the long spyglass. I closed my left eye and used my other to stare through the lens. At first I didn't see anything, but then I was able to make out what looked to be an island that was made out of thousands and thousands of brown trees.

"That's very strange. That looks like an island of old trees."

Salty took the spyglass back and scanned the ocean. "You mean *dead* trees, Ryder, dead Christmas trees to be exact. That is Dead Tree Island. That is where the Holiday Pirates store their treasures."

"Oh, cheese and crackers with hot sauce! Santa told us about the Holiday Pirates. He says they are to be feared." Jay the Elf put his hands on his head.

"Oh yes, I was warned about them in Santa Seal class!" Bob exclaimed.

"Santa is right. That's why I avoid sailing this way. I must've made a mistake." Salty tapped his stick against the deck.

I felt my heart sink. "No, I was the one at the wheel. I probably stopped paying attention. That's why we sailed off course. I'm sorry."

"That's OK, Master Ryder. We can make it through this situation."

"So what makes the Holiday Pirates so terrible?" Jay asked.

"Whatever holiday is being celebrated, the Holiday Pirates try to steal any part of the joy it brings people. They think if they can do that it will make them happy but it never does," Zandra quietly answered.

"Any holiday?" I asked.

"Yes," Zandra continued, "this isn't just about Christmas. This is about respecting everyone's beliefs and traditions. The Holiday Pirates don't respect anyone. They are miserable pirates. That is why Santa closed down that cave years back, and now there is another problem—the burning coal in the cave. That means. . . . This is not good. You see, those are coal dust clouds that cover their island."

"Do the pirates burn coal there?" I asked.

Zandra and Salty exchanged worried glances.

"What?" I asked.

"Well, Ryder." Zandra paused. "Not too far beyond *Dead Tree Island* there is the mainland that is connected to the North Pole."

"Well, that's good news, right?"

"Not exactly. That is where the coal burns. You see, what resides there is. . . ."

"Oh, no." Salty lowered his spyglass and said, "Just as I suspected. I see a Jolly Roger flying proudly and it's headed this way."

"Jolly Roger?" I asked and tried to put it together. "Wait, you mean Jolly Old Saint Nick? What's wrong with that? That's a good thing!"

Salty handed me the spyglass and shouted, "No! Not Jolly Old Saint Nick! A Jolly Roger! Look!"

I looked through the spyglass and spotted a ship sailing our way. Flying from the mast was a black flag showing the white skull and crossbones that told me one thing—HOLIDAY PIRATES!

"Oh, no," I said, and realized that the black clouds had grown, and I couldn't see anyone around me.

"Everyone! Down below!" Salty ordered, and I could hear Jay, Zandra, and Bob all shuffling about.

I was about to follow them when I heard a voice whisper in my ear, "Not so fast, mate! You're coming with me!"

I turned around and all I could make out was the outline of what I thought was a small man carrying a sword.

"Ryder! Ryder!" Zandra yelled, but her voice was now somewhere in the distance.

"Don't breathe a word." The sword moved closer to my nose.

"Wh . . . wh . . . whydah you want from me?" I was barely able to whisper.

"Whydah? Eh? Ah, I see, *The Whydah* is a Cape Cod ship so my guess is you're a Cape Cod pirate then?"

"Huh? What are you talking about?"

I heard Salty yell out, "Ryder, wherever you are, it looks like they anchored the ship! Beware of the rowboats!"

The pirate laughed and pointed his sword at the balcony. "Hurry up. Just go down that rope. You're going with me back to my ship."

I had no choice so I lowered myself down and got into the row boat that was tied to the *Aislynn*.

I could see the outline of the small man untying

135

the rope but still I wasn't able to make out his face or anything else for that matter, as he ordered me to row toward his ship. By the sound of his squeaky voice, I figured he must be young. Finally, when we were only yards from his ship, there was a break in the coal clouds and that's when I got a clear look at the face of the evil Holiday Pirate who had just kidnapped me. There was only one way to respond when I saw that face—LAUGH!!! AND LAUGH AND LAUGH!!

There before my eyes was a little boy around six or seven years old wearing a red stocking on his head and threatening me with a gray, *plastic* sword.

"What are you doing?" He pressed the tip against my neck, causing me to laugh so much that I put the oars aside and tried wiping my eyes dry.

"I'm sorry. Really, I don't mean to laugh," I said, trying to get serious, "but after everything I've been through. I mean. . . . C'mon, you're a little boy. Why should I be afraid of you?"

"How dare you, prisoner, laugh at me? I'm *not* a little boy. I'm a pirate! A Holiday Pirate! My name is Horatio Red Stocking, and I am the new captain of that ship, *The Jaded Dream*. So you will show me some respect, prisoner."

I realized he *was* serious and I also realized something else he had said and I didn't like it.

"Why should I respect you, Captain Red Stocking?"

"Ahhm, because you are my prisoner, that is why you should respect me!"

"People who try to make other people afraid don't deserve respect. Now, if you treated me right, like a friend does, then you would get my respect."

He thought for a minute and then said, "Really?"

"Yes. Really! And that toy sword you are holding isn't going to scare me, either."

He looked down at the sword and back up at me. "Toy sword? What's a toy?"

"You don't know what a toy is?" I asked in shock.

"No. The other pirates never told me."

"A toy is something you use when you play."

"Play? What does that word *play* mean?"

I couldn't believe what I was hearing, and thought before saying, "Actually, you're kind of playing right now. You're pretending you're a mean pirate but I don't think you are. I think you are only playing because, Horatio, I bet you're really a good kid. Are you?"

"I don't know. What happens to good kids?"

"Well, first of all, that red stocking you're wearing on your head wouldn't be on your head. You'd hang it by your fireplace and then on Christmas Eve, Santa would come down the chimney and fill up that stocking with toys and candy. You do know about candy, right?"

"Yes, I love candy, but I haven't had any since the

other pirates have left."

"You mean you are alone?"

"Yes. They all went to the North Pole. They planned on doing some pirating there, but I couldn't go because I was the youngest. I have been on *Dead Tree Island* for a while now. I thought if I took you prisoner, you could become a Holiday Pirate like me because I really don't know what I'm supposed to be doing as a pirate."

"Horatio, you're not supposed to be a pirate. You're supposed to be a kid, and instead of being your prisoner or a Holiday Pirate, I'd rather be your friend."

Horatio looked at me, confused.

I put out my hand. "My name is Ryder."

He looked at my hand and finally shook it and smiled. "Horatio."

It was at that point I realized the *Aislynn* was nowhere in sight, and then I noticed the red and gold Santa bag beside Horatio.

"Horatio, you stole the bag!" I exclaimed.

"Yes, I'm sorry, Ryder. That's what the Holiday Pirates taught me to do. But I don't want to be like them anymore. I want to be a good kid." He began to hand the bag to me but then I smiled and waved him off.

"That is Santa's bag, so how about you sail us to the North Pole and hand it to him yourself?"

"That sounds like a good idea. But who is this Santa you keep talking about? And what is Christmas?"

I laughed. "Let's get on the ship. It's a long story!"

We pulled up the anchor and I told Horatio all about Santa as he steered us toward the North Pole. Naturally, he was pretty amazed at the new world of Santa Claus that I described to him, but then suddenly we smacked right into land.

We got off the ship and began hiking across the windy and empty frozen land. It was getting dark, and I felt like we were walking around in endless circles, but then Horatio pointed. "Look up ahead. It's a sign."

We sprinted through the snow until we reached a big wooden sign with red lettering:

BEWARE

YOU ARE ENTERING THE VALLEY OF THE FRIGID SOULS!

"I `can't read. What does it say?" Horatio asked.

"Maybe you're better off not knowing," I replied.

"No, please, tell me!"

After I told Horatio, he looked at me. "Well, if *Santa's Village* is as magical as you say it is, it would be well worth the trip. So, let's go find out, Ryder!"

With Santa's bag slung over his shoulder, Horatio pushed on and I followed. We walked for a few minutes when we saw what looked to be several separate fires in the distance.

"What do you think that is?" I asked Horatio. Then I heard yelling coming from behind us.

"Ryder! Ryder! Ryder!" It was Zandra, Bob, and Jay.

Horatio turned to me. "Are those seals really talking to you?"

I smiled. "You understand them. Horatio, I knew you were a good kid!"

Jay ran ahead of the pack and grabbed my arm. "Ryder, you have to turn around! Now!"

"OK, but why do we have to go?"

"They're coming!" He pointed at the fires that now seemed to be moving.

"Who?"

"The Coal Monsters!" he hollered, pointing at the red fires that I realized were more than just fires. There was nothing *frigid* about the valley, as hundreds of monsters made from burning red coals headed straight for me! They moved slowly but they really didn't have to run because I couldn't move. I was in shock. I had never been so frightened in my life!

"We have to go! We have to go now!" Jay tugged on my arm, and out of the corner of my eye, I saw Horatio shoot past me and run toward Zandra and Bob.

Part of me screamed, "Run!" but the other part of me had a question that burned inside me as hot as the Coal Monsters.

"Jay," I shouted to him, keeping my eyes on the monsters, "tell me, is *Santa's Village* beyond those monsters?"

Jay was still tugging on my arm. "Yes, but we have to go! Now!"

"No," I heard myself say. "We have to get the seals and the bag to Santa."

Even though I was afraid, I thought of what my friend the Old Hag had said to me when she talked about the bullies at school: "You can't always go out the back door. There will be a time when you'll have to face them." I knew that now was the time.

I shook Jay's hand away, gritted my teeth, and sprinted as hard as I could toward the monsters. They instantly surrounded me and the heat from their red coals made me sweat, causing my heart to pound like a jackhammer.

"Don't be afraid, Ryder!" I said to myself, and moved forward. And then I was face to face with the biggest Coal Monster. I could see that his eyes weren't burning like the rest of him. In fact, they looked wide-eyed and scared and a lot like my eyes had been during my journey. But during my secret journey, I had learned many things and one was that fear was a feeling that I would no longer let control me.

"I am not afraid of you!" I shouted. "I actually feel sorry for you because *you* are the one who really is afraid. You, Mr. Coal Monster, are afraid of what the other Coal Monsters will think about you, and because of that fear you are not being who you are meant to be. You *can* be good. I know you can. I know all of you can!"

All of the Coal Monsters then looked at one another and nodded and then one of the most amazing things happened. The coals began to burn out, and transformed into diamonds. Then one by one the diamonds fell off the monsters, exposing what they really were—boys and girls!

"You saved us! You saved us!" the biggest kid said to me. He looked a lot like one of the fourth-grade bullies from my school, except one thing made him different. He seemed happy.

Jay, Horatio, Bob, and Zandra all hurried over to me. "You did it, Ryder!"

"You faced them!" Bob said.

Zandra hugged me with her fins and whispered, "You faced your fears."

"So what will we do with all of the diamonds?" Jay asked.

Horatio raised his hand. "I think we should give them to Santa so he can have money to buy supplies to build toys for *all* boys and girls."

All the former Coal Monsters and I cheered, lifting Horatio on our shoulders, but then we stopped when we heard the sound of jingling bells in the distance. The bells got louder and the sound of squawks was followed by meows and barks. Then I saw it! Coming into the valley were thirteen cats, six dogs, and a bird named Raven Ron who was leading the way for Santa Claus. Santa was directing a horse-drawn sleigh, and in the sleigh beside him was none other than the Old Hag herself! But she looked different. She wasn't an Old Hag at all. She wore a matching red Santa suit and looked as beautiful as. . . .

"Mrs. Claus," Santa said to her, "I have to admit, your plan worked brilliantly. Look at all the good children that are now here thanks to you giving the key to Ryder." Santa chuckled.

"Mrs. Claus?!" I said.

Jay patted me on the back. "Sorry, Ryder, I was sworn to secrecy."

"The night you cried about wanting to be an elf?" I asked Jay.

"No, those were real tears, alright. I didn't know it was Mrs. Claus staying near your house and I definitely didn't know her plan until after Dr. Phocas took the submarine and went after you."

"And *believe* us, we didn't know about *any* plan at all!" Bob said, and Zandra nodded.

"You see, Ryder," Santa said as he helped Mrs. Claus out of the sleigh, "we needed a good child to help these children to see that they could be good themselves."

"The bonus was that you also helped Dr. Phocas," Mrs. Claus said and added, "and you yourself became who you are meant to be. You see, just before Christmas every year I go to your neighborhood and so many others to find out who's been naughty or nice and then I report back to Santa. I am getting a bit tired of it and realized, Ryder, you might be able to help some children discover how good they can be. I hope you're not mad at me."

I laughed. "Of course I'm not mad, Mrs. Claus, but I do want to know one thing."

"What is that?" Mrs. Claus asked.

"What *did* O'Nel want for Christmas?"

They both laughed, and Mrs. Claus said, "You'll have to find that out in the Epilogue of this story."

"The Ep-i-what?"

"You'll see soon enough," Santa said to me, and turned to the group. "Now, everyone, let's get into the sleigh and head back to the village. We have a very special Christmas to prepare for! After all, this is going to be Horatio's very first Christmas!"

Horatio ran over, gave Santa his bag, and hugged him while everyone cheered and piled into the sleigh.

I laughed as Santa sat up front and was then surrounded by the thirteen cats, six dogs, and Raven Ron, who also jumped in!

"You and your pets, Mrs. Claus," Santa said.

"Oh, they're fun. They keep me company when I'm away from you working on the Naughty or Nice list." A brown Great Dane dog licked Santa's face.

"No more pets, Mrs. Claus!" Santa grumbled again, but then chuckled as Raven Ron squawked along to the Christmas carols everyone sang all the way back to Santa's Village!

Epilogue

After Santa gave me a tour of his village, he explained what an epilogue is.

"Ever hear of a baker's dozen, Ryder?" he asked.

"Yeah, that's when the baker throws in an extra cookie or muffin when someone orders a dozen."

"Exactly, it's that extra treat. That's what an epilogue is in a story. It's that extra something," Santa said, and punched some numbers and a door swooshed open.

"OK." I nodded.

"By the way, good work on cracking my code for the lock on the *Aislynn*," he said, walking into the room.

"Thanks, Santa."

"Anyway, in this case, Ryder, your epilogue begins here." Santa smiled and I followed him into a room that had thousands and thousands of toys that I had never seen before.

"Santa's Secret Toy Room," I gasped.

Santa's brow rose. "You know about my secret toy room?"

"Jay kind of let it slip."

"Cheese and crackers with gingerbread men!" Santa said.

I laughed. "Please, don't be mad at him."

"Hey, any elf who can drive a truck with only three wheels is a pretty good elf in my book. Tonight I'm even going to let him drive the sleigh for a little while."

"Tonight?"

"Oh, that's right. You've probably lost track of time. Tonight is Christmas Eve."

"Oh, no, Santa, I have to get home! My parents are coming to my uncle's house and if I'm not there. . . ."

"Slow down." He waved his hands. "We will have you home in plenty of time. Now, since you saved the seals, Dr. Phocas, and all of those wonderful children, I thought you should be allowed into this room to pick out your Christmas gift."

My eyes bugged out. "Really, Santa?"

"Yes. You can pick any gift. It can even be a gift that I will be giving children in the future."

I ran around the room and played with all different types of toys—toys I had never seen before! I narrowed my search to three choices—a skateboard with a rocket, a bicycle that could be driven on air and water, and sunglasses that when worn allow you to see aliens in outer space!

I didn't know which one to pick and that's when I saw it—my ultimate Christmas gift! A gift that could last forever! I picked it up and inspected it before handing it to Santa.

"Can you put this under my uncle's tree? I'm staying at his place."

Santa chuckled. "I know you are staying at Uncle Ted's place. I don't know how I do it but I know these things. . . ." He paused and looked again at what I had picked for my gift. "Ryder, I was really hoping that you would pick this. I promise it will be under your tree when you wake up. But now I have to ask you for a favor." He offered me the red and gold Christmas bag.

"What's the bag for, Santa?"

"Ryder, before I drop you home, could you carry this bag and swim with Zandra and Bob? I have a very big delivery to make and I could use your help."

With his other hand, Santa pointed at a water slide in the corner of the room. Above it was a sign that read—SANTA'S NORTH POLE ENTRANCE.

"Sometimes I like to go scuba diving in the caves during the off season," he said.

"Wow!"

"So, if you go down that slide it will take you to Zandra and Bob and the Ocean Elves. They're waiting for you. So, will you do that for me?"

Santa didn't have to ask twice. I put my mask on,

saluted, clutched the bag, and dove down the slide face first. In seconds, I was traveling like a human rocket through a clear water tube that zigzagged hundreds of miles under the North Pole until it finally shot me out into the open ocean.

With some Ocean Elves trailing, Zandra and Bob swam over to me.

"Santa never lets any of us come down here that way," one of the Ocean Elves pouted.

"Well, Ryder's been a good boy." Zandra smiled at me. "OK, everyone let's go! We have a special gift to drop off first."

I followed closely behind as we swam through the pearl-lit caves that changed to bright colors from the jellyfish. I wanted the moment to last forever, but in seconds we were at our stop.

When I came out of the ocean, Santa was already waiting for me on a warm beach. "Did you have fun?" he asked.

"Yes. That was better than any waterslide in the world. . . . Where am I?" I asked.

"You're in Jamaica, little Ryder man." O'Nel came off Santa's sleigh.

"O'Nel!" I ran over and hugged him as Santa took the bag from me and said, "Move back, everyone!"

"You always wondered what I wanted for Christmas," O'Nel said, and pointed over to Santa, who climbed into the bag, which suddenly grew and became as large as a truck! Then I realized it *was* a truck as Santa drove a green, yellow, and red ice cream truck out of the bag, parked it, and threw the keys to O'Nel.

"Thanks so much, Santa! The children in my neighborhood will love it."

Santa laughed. "No problem at all, O'Nel. You've had this wish for many years. I've just waited for the right time to grant it. You truly understand the meaning of Christmas! And also, if it wasn't for your name, I think Ryder would still be trying to open that lock on the *Aislynn!*"

We all laughed and said goodbye to O'Nel as he drove away.

"Well, Ryder, it's time Santa dropped you home," Bob said.

"Yes, we will miss you, Ryder," Zandra added, and they both hugged me.

"I'll never forget you." I wiped my tears away with my sleeve.

"We believe you." Zandra kissed my forehead and both of them slipped back into the ocean.

I climbed back onto the sleigh and suddenly my eyes felt heavy. The last thing I remember hearing was, "Cheese and crackers with eggnog! Hurry up, Jay, we have to get Ryder home!"

"Hey, Santa, cheese and crackers is my line!" Jay replied,

but before I could laugh I felt my eyes get even heavier and a part of me knew I was already sound asleep.

"Are you going to sleep the day away?" I heard a voice ask, and it was my dad.

I propped my head up and looked around. "Where's Santa?"

"Well, it's Christmas. He's already been here, sleepyhead." My mom stood beside Dad, smiling.

I rubbed my eyes. Was it a dream? Was the whole thing a dream? Please don't let it be a dream, I thought. But then Dad asked me one of the best questions I had ever heard!

"Hey, Ryder, Buddy, where did you get those cool-looking pajamas?"

I looked down at the white O and E on my chest.

"*Yes*! It did happen! That means Santa really did come!"

I hopped down the stairs three at a time, ran over to the Christmas tree, and looked for the gift that read, To Ryder and Uncle Ted From Santa.

I picked it up and ran over to my uncle and handed it to him.

"This is for both of us. It's from Santa. Open it up, Uncle Ted."

Uncle Ted put his coffee mug down and unwrapped the paper.

It was a book with the title *SAVING SANTA'S SEALS*.

"Remember you once told me there was nothing more meaningful to the world than a good story because it's a gift you leave future boys and girls?"

"Yes." He smiled.

"The story of Saving Santa's Seals is the best gift Santa and Mrs. Claus could have ever given us because it will now be the gift we can leave for future boys and girls."

"You are so right, my smart little nephew."

My mom took the book and opened it and said, "What kind of book is this? All of the pages are empty!"

"Not for long," Uncle Ted replied, laughing with me. "Did I tell you Ryder was a big help? I don't have writer's block anymore."

"How did he cure it?" Dad asked, now thumbing through the blank book.

"Ryder reminded me how much I love writing stories for children. And, as much as they try, I can't ever let the Coal Monsters of this world make me forget that I am a storyteller. I'm Storyteller Ted. Isn't that right, Ryder?"

"That's right," I laughed. "Wait a second, the Coal Monsters? How do you know about them? You had already gone home when that part of the story happened to me."

"I have my ways, and maybe in real life I *had* gone home but who knows what will happen in the book? I might even want to be a hero just like you, my little nephew." Uncle Ted saluted and chuckled.

"Well, I will help you then. It will be my mission!" I saluted back and we both laughed for a very long time!

THE END ... OR IS IT?

My Very Own Christmas Story

by _____

_____

_____

_____

_____

_____

_____

_____

_____

_____

_____

_____

_____

My Very Own Christmas Story

My Very Own Christmas Story

MY VERY OWN CHRISTMAS STORY

_____

_____

_____

_____

_____

_____

_____

_____

_____

_____

_____

_____

_____

_____

_____

Acknowledgments

I would like to thank some of the many people who have been there for me during the down times—Vanessa Andrade, Judge William McCarthy, Matt and Kristen Curran, Sean and Beth Keating, Dennis and Amy Gilligan, Dave and Keri Stack, Todd and Jay Oliveira, Craig and Kenny Kozens, Paula Kapulka, Seth Thomas, Andrea Norris, Sarah Vallely, Jeff and Ali Gonsalves, Scott and Nicole Etler, Susan Nabreski, Kathy Hoyle, Kerry Williams, Chris and Tammy Mathews, O'Nel Headley, the Cox family, Derrick and Jenny Nelson, Greg Papasodora, Amy Sullivan, Buddy Bess, Mike Metzler, Patrick and Melissa Clancy, Peter Tolan, my creative writing students, my brother Seton, and my sisters Nina, Joanna, Sarah, and Courtney.

I would also like to thank Gerald Hagerty for being a true friend, my lawyer Jeffrey Wolf for being a man of integrity who looks out for the little guy, John Furfey for creating my Web site www.CapeCodWriter.com, my uncle Jack Matthews for making every Christmas for the Murphys so bright, my nephew Ryder Ferris for inspiring me, Rob Taylor for being a friend and a trusted business partner whose persistence and dedication to this book brought it from an idea to reality, Adam Taylor for his tremendous talent, Lisa and Michael Graziano of Leapfrog Press for believing in this book, and Ed Murphy for being an extremely generous friend over the years!

The Author

T.M. Murphy, featured in the new book *101 Highly Successful Novelists*, is the author of the Belltown Mystery series, listed as a Favorite New Series by BookSense Children's 76. Murphy spends his days touring schools, motivating kids to write, and teaching young writers during the summer at The Writers' Shack in his hometown. Please visit him with your stories about Christmas at www. CapeCodWriter.com.

The Illustrator

Adam Taylor's diversified illustration and animation talent has appeared in television, film, publishing, and the Internet, with projects for MGM Studios, Disney, Virgin Records, CBS, and National Geographic Kids. Please visit him at www.taylorentertaiment.com.

About the Type

This book was set in Adobe Caslon, a typeface originally released by William Caslon in 1722. His types became popular throughout Europe and the American colonies, and printer Benjamin Franklin used hardly any other typeface. The first printings of the American Declaration of Independence and the Constitution were set in Caslon. For her Caslon revival for Adobe, designer Carol Twombly studied specimen pages printed by William Caslon between 1734 and 1770.

Designed by John Taylor-Convery
Composed at JTC Imagineering, Santa Maria, CA